It Shouldn't Have Been Like This....

It should have been them getting naked together. Not him shucking his clothes while Cait bustled around like some damned efficient nurse, filling a plastic bag with ice and tapping her foot and looking as if she had a hot date in half an hour.

Okay, so she *was* a nurse.

But she wasn't indifferent. She loved him, for crying out loud! She'd stroked and touched his body in ways that had made his heart gallop and his body sing.

And now she was acting as if he were a floor she'd been hired to scrub.

Yeah, well, let's see how long her indifference lasted.

"Where exactly does it hurt?" she asked. "Here?" She put her hand on his thigh, kneading it gently. Then she slid her hand beneath his leg, probing lightly. "I can feel the tension here."

Charlie stifled a moan. "Ah…um…yeah, there." His fingers clenched against the table. He shut his eyes and threw his head back.

She lifted his leg and slid the ice pack under it, then went back to fill another.

Charlie felt cold and bereft. His body didn't want more ice. It wanted Cait.…

Dear Reader,

Welcome to Silhouette Desire! We're delighted to offer you again this month six passionate, powerful and provocative romances sure to please you.

Start with December's fabulous MAN OF THE MONTH, *A Cowboy's Promise.* This latest title in Anne McAllister's popular CODE OF THE WEST miniseries features a rugged Native American determined to win back the woman he left three years before. Then discover *The Secret Life of Connor Monahan* in Elizabeth Bevarly's tale of a vice cop who mistakenly surmises that a prim and proper restaurateur is operating a call-girl ring.

The sizzling miniseries 20 AMBER COURT concludes with Anne Marie Winston's *Risqué Business*, in which a loyal employee tries to prevent a powerful CEO with revenge on his mind from taking over the company she thinks of as her family. Reader favorite Maureen Child delivers the next installment of another exciting miniseries, THE FORTUNES OF TEXAS: THE LOST HEIRS. In *Did You Say Twins?!* a marine sergeant inherits twin daughters and is forced to turn for help to the woman who refused his marriage proposal ten years before.

The sexy hero of *Michael's Temptation,* the last book in Eileen Wilks's TALL, DARK & ELIGIBLE miniseries, goes to Central America to rescue a lovely lady who's been captured by guerrillas. And sparks fly when a smooth charmer and a sassy tomboy are brought together by their shared inheritance of an Australian horse farm in Brownyn Jameson's *Addicted to Nick.*

Take time out from the holiday rush and treat yourself to all six of these not-to-be-missed romances.

Enjoy,

Joan Marlow Golan

Joan Marlow Golan
Senior Editor, Silhouette Desire

A Cowboy's Promise

ANNE McALLISTER

Silhouette®

Desire®

Published by Silhouette Books
America's Publisher of Contemporary Romance

SILHOUETTE BOOKS

ISBN 0-373-76405-7

A COWBOY'S PROMISE

This edition published by arrangement with Harlequin Books S.A.

Visit Silhouette at www.eHarlequin.com

Printed in U.S.A.

Books by Anne McAllister

Silhouette Desire

**Cowboys Don't Cry* #907
**Cowboys Don't Quit* #944
**Cowboys Don't Stay* #969
**The Cowboy and the Kid* #1009
**Cowboy Pride* #1034
**The Cowboy Steals a Lady* #1117
**The Cowboy Crashes a Wedding* #1153
**The Stardust Cowboy* #1219
**A Cowboy's Secret* #1279
Blood Brothers #1307
**A Cowboy's Promise* #1405

Silhouette Special Edition

**A Cowboy's Tears* #1137

Silhouette Books

World's Most Eligible Bachelors
**Cowboy on the Run*

*Code of the West

ANNE MCALLISTER

RITA Award-winning author Anne McAllister fell in love with a cowboy when she was five years old. Tall, dark, handsome, lone-wolf types have appealed to her ever since. "Me, for instance," her college-professor husband says. Well, yes. But even though she's been married to the man of her dreams for over thirty years, she still likes writing about those men of the West! And even though she may take a break from cowboy heroes now and then, she has lots more stories planned for the CODE OF THE WEST. She is always happy to hear from readers, and if you'd like, you can write to Anne at P.O. Box 3904, Bozeman, Montana 59772. SASE appreciated. And you can visit her Web site at www.annemcallister.com and e-mail Anne your comments to anne@annemcallister.com.

For my stepfather,
John J. Perkins
(1917–2000)

Who taught me that love is thicker than blood

Prologue

They said that hearing was the last sense to go.

His hadn't gone. Yet.

But the light was getting brighter. He could see it, could see shapes in the distance—people—silhouetted in front of it. He tried to move closer.

"Hold him still, damn it!" The harsh voice came from a long way away.

"I'm trying! I'm trying!" That voice, too, barely penetrated his consciousness.

"C'mon! He's losin' a lot of blood. Must've took three bullets at least. Hurry up!"

"I'm moving as fast as I can!"

"Well, move faster! We don't get him there soon, he ain't gonna make it."

The light grew brighter, then dimmed. The voices muttered on, the noises grew harsher. He could hear metal on metal. Clanking. Jostling.

"Here. Just shove the door open. Give me that!"

"He's bleeding all over the place!"

"Press down, damn it!"

"I am!"

The light was brighter again. The faces clearer.

He could make out features. He could see his father.

Was that his father? That young smiling man? God, it had been years. He'd been three when the old man died. And his vague last memories of his father had not been of a happy man.

But he was happy now—with Charlie's mother, both of them smiling, their arms around each other and around Lucy, too. His mom had died when he was ten; his sister, five years later.

Luce, damn it, how could you have got yourself killed like that?

He moved closer into the light and tried to call out.

"We're losin' him!"

"I know! I know! Come on!"

Charlie barely heard the voices now. They didn't matter. He was trying to reach Lucy.

He had so much to tell her—about everything that had happened since she'd gone—about Joanna, her teacher, who had taken him on, had kicked his butt, determined not to let him die in the streets the way his sister had, about Chase, Joanna's husband, who had taught him how to be a man.

But before he could speak, he saw more faces.

He saw Chase and Joanna. He saw their children, Emerson, Alex and Annie, who had become like little brothers and sister to him.

Whoa. Wait a sec. *They* weren't dead! None of them!

Then what—

Charlie looked around, puzzled.

He scanned the faces. He saw his best friend, Herbert,

from grammar school and DeShayne and Lopez, the guys he had hung with in high school, all still alive and kicking as far as he knew. He saw Gaby, his agent, who he'd spoken to last week, and his old friends Miles and Susan Cavanaugh and their sons, Patrick and James.

His gaze swept over them all. And moved on.

He was looking for one face.

One woman.

Where was she?

Cait!

He called her name. But no one replied.

Cait!

Everyone—his father, his mother, his sister, his friends—all stood silent and looked back at him blankly.

He reached them now, and the light was all around him. But he barely noticed. Instead of greeting his family, instead of throwing his arms around them in the joy of reunion, he pushed past them, wildly looking around.

Cait!

Silence. Emptiness.

She wasn't here.

He was going to die and she wasn't going to be a part of his eternity?

Of course she wasn't, he realized.

How could she be when he hadn't let her be a part of his life?

One

Abuk, Western Asia

The hospital wasn't there.

There was a pile of rubble instead.

The taxi driver who had brought him here shook his head. "I told you so."

At least Charlie guessed that was the meaning of the words the man was saying over and over. He'd given the driver the name of the hospital as soon as he'd limped out of the airport. And the driver had protested then.

"No, no. Can't go. Not there," he'd said over and over.

But Charlie had insisted. He hadn't come halfway around the world to be turned back three miles from his goal.

He hadn't realized then that "not there," meant the hospital itself.

The heat was suffocating, making him feel even dizzier

and weaker than he was. He'd left Los Angeles twenty odd hours ago, had killed time in Amsterdam and more in Istanbul before the long final flight into Abuk.

He was doing the whole trip against doctors' orders. A whole roomful of white-coated medicos had told him he wasn't ready for anything strenuous.

"You coded," one of them told him bluntly. "Clinically you were dead. You lost quarts of blood. You can barely walk. You aren't going to get better traipsing halfway around the world."

Yes, Charlie thought. He was.

He was doing the one thing that was going to make him really better at last. He was going to make up for lost time. He was going to find Cait.

The thought of Cait was what had got him through all the rehab he'd done so far.

"Where are the other hospitals?"

The driver gestured this way and that, and finally ended up pointing in two directions.

Charlie tried to remember which would be the more likely choice. He flipped through his pocket dictionary and found the word for *near*. Then he fished a wad of local notes out of his pocket and said it.

The driver nodded, pocketed the money happily, and off they jolted once more.

The city had changed in two years. The war that wasn't called a war had died down. When Charlie had been here last, it had been in full swing—sniping and strafing had been the order of the day.

No lines had been drawn. There were no clear "sides." You took your life in your hands whenever you ventured out. And you were as likely to have been killed by one faction as another. Misery had been everywhere.

It pretty much still was.

Two years ago Charlie had come to photograph it. It

was his job, and he did it well. He found pain and heartache and inhumanity wherever it existed, exposed it in black-and-white, then showed it to the world.

For five years he'd done a spectacular job doing just that. His photos had been hung from Paris to L.A. They'd found their way into private collections and galleries all over the world. His book of photo essays, *Inhumanity,* which had contained, among other things, two sets of photos taken right here, had become a bestseller this past spring while he was still in the hospital.

It was what damned near getting killed did for you.

"Nonsense," he remembered his agent Gabriela del Castillo saying, her green eyes flashing angrily at his deliberate irreverence. "Your book is selling because it touches people. You find the heart of things, Charlie. You challenge the soul."

"And getting three bullets in me didn't hurt."

"Didn't hurt? They nearly killed you!" Gaby had been furious about his being in the wrong place at the wrong time when he'd got caught in that Middle-East crossfire. "I worry about you."

"You should be glad," Charlie had maintained. "It boosted sales."

"I'm not that mercenary," Gaby retorted. "Truly. I worry. I don't know why you aren't dead."

Charlie knew.

Because he couldn't spend eternity without Cait.

He hadn't said so to Gaby. He hadn't said so to anyone. He hadn't talked about it at all.

Talking about eternity and near-death experiences wasn't something he did.

To Gaby and everyone else, Charlie Seeks Elk was a gutsy, earthy, hard-nosed pragmatist, the embodiment of the what-you-see-is-what-you-get guy. Down-to-earth realism was the name of his game. Charlie was the last man on earth given to out-of-body experiences, to messages from the other side.

But the day he'd been shot—the day he'd coded—he had seen a bright light. He'd seen his family—all of them dead for years. He'd seen his friends, and knew the promise that they would spend eternity together. And frankly, he'd have been happy to join them.

But not if Cait wasn't there.

When he'd left her two years ago, turning his back on the idea of marriage and family, he'd done it for both their sakes. He'd felt strong, noble, independent—a man with a cause who couldn't be tied down.

But that was before he'd faced eternity—without the prospect of Cait.

It surprised him how instinctively he'd looked for her. He hadn't known he would. But he hadn't ever died before.

Since he had, he knew what mattered.

And he had to find Cait.

The driver whipped through semideserted avenues lined with rubble and burned-out buildings, heading back toward a more populated area of town. This part had been heavily populated when he'd been here. They drove right past the building where Charlie had rented a room, where he had taken Cait in his arms, where she had taken him into her body. There was nothing there now but two half walls and a pile of crumbling stucco. Charlie shut his eyes and prayed.

When he opened them again he saw a section of the street where the rubble had been cleared away. A foundation was being dug for a new building. The taxi driver was saying something, smiling, pointing and nodding.

Charlie caught a few words. *Peace. New. Hope.*

There was nothing there yet but a hole in the ground. But if you dared believe, it was a harbinger of hope, a belief in a future where buildings would be allowed to stand, where families would thrive again, where children would live unmaimed.

"Yes," he said. "Yes." And he leaned his head back against the sticky plastic upholstery of the car and hoped, too.

He hoped that at the next hospital, he'd find Cait.

But she wasn't there.

The health organization she worked for had pulled out, the director told him. "They come in during emergencies," the man said in heavily accented English, smiling at Charlie across the counter. "You see we are not emergent anymore."

Charlie wasn't seeing much of anything. He clung to the countertop to keep himself upright. His head was spinning. His leg throbbed.

"What about another hospital. She wouldn't be at another hospital here?"

"Not unless she left her job and stayed." The man shook his head. "You have to have a good reason to stay."

She might have had a reason. "What about the orphans?" Charlie asked urgently.

The man looked perplexed. "Orphans?"

"There were children at that hospital." Charlie's knuckles were white against the counter. "Kids who'd been hurt. Kids without families. Kids abandoned. If she'd wanted to adopt one..."

She *had* wanted to adopt one—a four-year-old girl with a shattered arm and the most expressive dark eyes Charlie had ever seen. Resi.

The director steepled his fingers. "I do not know of orphans." He pulled out a file and consulted it, then gave Charlie three addresses. "You will have to go there and check."

Clutching the piece of paper, Charlie left. He needed sleep. He needed pain medication.

More, he needed to find Cait.

He found another taxi. He gave the driver the addresses. They went from one orphanage to another. At each one Charlie described the little girl, Resi. At each he asked about the American nurse, Cait Blasingame. At all of them he was met with sad smiles and commiserations.

"No, I am sorry."

"No, no one like that here."

"No. We have never heard of them."

No Resi. No Cait.

For three days he stayed in Abuk and he searched. He went to every hospital, every clinic, every doctor's surgery he could find. He went to the consulate. He went to the newspapers. He went everywhere he could think of.

If Cait was here, he would find her.

In the end he was sick. In the end he was fevered. In the end he had to admit she was gone.

It had been a long shot, of course. He hadn't admitted that to himself before.

All the time he'd been recovering, he'd focused on getting well enough to go back to Abuk to find Cait, to say the words he'd never wanted to say before.

Marry me.

For three months he'd hoped and dreamed and planned. He had promised himself he would find her and he hadn't let himself think beyond that.

Now he was here and Cait wasn't.

Now what?

"So," Gaby stared down at him in his hospital bed, her expression a mixture of concern and irritation, "were they worth it?"

"Were what worth it?" Charlie didn't want company.

He'd told the nurse that. He had been turning away visitors since he'd ended up here a week ago after returning to L.A.

But Gaby never listened to nurses. Gaby was convinced she knew better than anyone. Now she loomed over him like a blond-haired avenging angel, ready to do mayhem. "The photos you had to go halfway around the world to take!"

Charlie turned his head toward the wall. "I didn't take any photos."

There was complete, stunned silence. Charlie lived to take photos. If he didn't take photos, Gaby used to say, he'd be dead.

Now, quietly, she asked, "So what did you go for, then?"

The old Charlie—the self-contained, fiercely independent Charlie—would have said, "Nothing." He would have stonewalled her the way he had stonewalled all attempts to invade his privacy for years.

But the new Charlie had a whole new perspective on life. Besides, he was so damn weak even now, after a full week of antibiotics and transfusions and hospital bed rest, that the stone wall was crumbling.

"I was trying to find someone," he muttered. His voice was low, and the words were hard to get out.

He hadn't said them to anyone. He hadn't even told his best friends, Chase and Joanna Whitelaw—the couple who had more or less become his surrogate parents when he was sixteen years old—about Cait.

He might have, but Chase and Joanna were gone.

Two weeks ago they had left for Europe for two months with their kids. It was a trip they'd been planning for a long time. Originally they'd planned to meet him in Athens. But that was before he'd got shot and sent home.

Then Joanna had been on the verge of canceling the whole trip. Charlie had argued against it.

He was home, he assured her. He was on the mend. He was fine! It wasn't merely that he wanted them to have the vacation they'd looked forward to for so long.

It was also that he'd wanted them gone so Joanna wouldn't fuss when he left to look for Cait.

They didn't know he had gone. They didn't know he was back. They didn't know he was in the hospital. And he had no intention of telling them.

But Gaby had caught him with his defenses down. If she'd bullied him, he might not have said any more, but Gaby knew when to bully and when to just wait. Now she waited. She pulled up a chair and sat beside the bed.

"Who matters that much?" Her voice was gentler than he'd ever heard it. She wrapped her fingers around his and gave a gentle squeeze.

He shook his head vaguely. "A friend," he said. "A woman I knew there. A nurse." He looked away. "Her name was Cait."

"Was?" There was a worried edge to Gaby's voice.

Charlie swallowed. "She's not dead. At least I don't think she is." God, he wouldn't let himself think anything like that! "She's just…gone."

"Gone where?"

"Don't know." He plucked at the coverlet, worrying it between his fingers. "She worked for one of those global medicine outfits, the ones who send personnel into war zones and disaster areas. It's still pretty much a disaster," he reflected, "but not an active one. So they've pulled out. I don't know where they are. Where she is."

"Have you asked?"

"Of course. I called from here. I might have had better luck if I'd stormed the headquarters. It was easy enough for them to tell me they don't give out that information.

Privacy, you know?'' His mouth twisted. He understood their concerns, but it didn't help him.

''Do you have an address for her family?''

''No. She was from Montana. She used to talk about it all the time. Used to call it 'the last best place.' I used to tell her that was a slogan, and she said it was truth in advertising.'' He smiled now at the thought.

In his mind he could still see Cait's own smile whenever they'd had that teasing exchange:

''You should see it, Charlie,'' she would say. ''You'd love it.''

And he'd shake his head in protest. ''No way. Not me. I'm a city boy.''

But she'd persist, telling him stories about the ranch where she'd grown up, about herding cattle and branding calves, about seeing bears and coyotes and, once, she thought, a wolf.

She told him about fishing in the creek and swimming in the swimming hole and training her horse and tagging along after her father or her older brother, Wes. And he let her talk because he liked watching her face whenever she told those stories. Her hazel eyes would get kind of soft and misty, and she would smile a sort of faraway, loving, gentle smile.

It was a childhood so unlike his own. Her memories were happy ones, so very unlike his.

''What was it like where you grew up?'' she'd asked him time and again.

But Charlie had just shaken his head and lied. ''I don't remember.''

Now he found that he remembered her stories even better than he remembered the things that had really happened to him.

''I'll look for her,'' Gaby said. ''I'll find out where she is. I'll get her to come and see you.''

"No!"

Gaby stared at him. "I thought you wanted to find her."

"I do, but...but I have to go to her." He knew that much. He would wait until hell froze over before Cait would ever come to him.

Gaby considered that. She considered him.

After the shooting, Gaby had come from Santa Fe to see him as soon as he'd been well enough to come back to Los Angeles.

He'd gone to his own apartment, refusing to stay at Chase and Joanna's, making it difficult for everyone, but needing the pretense that he was doing fine on his own.

Of course he hadn't been. Joanna had come and stayed with him. Or Chase had. Or one of the Cavanaughs. Patrick, who was fifteen now, and James, just turned thirteen, had even done their share of nursemaiding.

And then Gaby had come.

He remembered her sitting by his bed while he slept and, at other times, talking quietly, worriedly, with Chase and Joanna when they'd thought he couldn't hear. She'd been devoted on more than a business level, though Charlie had never asked for that.

Once, early in their professional relationship, in her straightforward way, Gaby had asked if he might someday be interested in more than that. In his own straightforward way, Charlie had said no. He knew she didn't mean an affair. Gaby was a marriage-minded woman. He had told her he wasn't ever getting married, that he would never care about any woman that way or that much.

She had taken him at his word. He wondered what she was thinking now, but he didn't wonder enough to ask.

He felt her hand squeeze his fingers.

"I'll look, Charlie," she said. "I'll be back to let you know what I find out."

* * *

Two days later, when he came in from physical therapy, Gaby was waiting for him.

''She's from rural Elmer, Montana,'' Gaby said without preamble. ''That's in the Shields Valley. Daughter of Walter Blasingame, owner of the Rafter WB Ranch, acreage unreportable because apparently it's bad form to inquire.'' Gaby rolled her eyes. ''She is presently nurse-midwife at a practice in Livingston. The nearest airport is Bozeman. If you want a place to stay, Brenna McCall has a cabin about half a mile from Blasingame's land.''

Charlie just leaned on his crutches and stared.

Gaby smiled brightly and shrugged. ''Anything else?''

''How did you do that?'' He was shaking his head, amazed, his heart quickening in his chest. ''She's there? In Montana? In Livingston?''

''Living with her father, Brenna says.''

''You talked to *Brenna* about her?'' It was one thing to bare his soul to Gaby. He didn't want the whole damn world knowing his business!

''I did not spill your guts,'' Gaby said indignantly. ''I checked the Internet for Blasingames in Montana. When I found out where they were, I started checking each one. When it turned out that one of them lived near Brenna, it seemed foolish not to check. I know Brenna. I hung a show for her in my gallery last year. You know her. She does those fantastic watercolor, pen-and-ink cowboys?''

Charlie nodded vaguely. He didn't remember. He didn't care. He could only think about Cait. Gaby had found Cait!

''Thanks.''

''You're welcome. You are not haring off, though,'' Gaby said firmly. ''This time before you take off anywhere, you are going to be fit.''

Charlie grinned. The world was brighter. Cait was in Montana. ''Yeah, sure. Whatever you say.''

* * *

“That’s it, Milly! Oh, good. Oh, yes. That’s right. Push. Keep going. Push, push, push!” Cait positioned herself to help ease the arrival of this new little person into the world. She could see lots of dark hair and a furrowed brow and then an entire fierce little face. She always loved this part, being there to witness the emergence of new life, to share in the first moments when a tiny new human being came into the world.

Milly Callahan, her fingers strangling those of her husband, Cash, was doing great. They were both doing great. “Just one more now,” Cait said. “Whenever you’re ready.”

And moments later a blinking, black-haired baby boy entered the world.

“He’s here!” Milly wept, her chin wavering, tears leaking down her cheeks and rolling into her ears.

“Ohmigod,” Cash said, tears and joy mingling on his face. “Ohmigod. I’ve got a son! Can you believe it? God, Mil’, look at him! He is so beautiful!”

They all were—scrawny, red and wet, there was nothing as beautiful as a newborn child. Cait, too, could have just sat and stared at him for hours, marveling at the miracle of life. But she had work to do, so it wasn’t until all the afterbirth business was taken care of, the baby checked over and Milly, too, that she allowed herself a moment to savor the glow of the family before her.

The child, now named Cash James after his father and henceforth to be called C.J., was swaddled in a blue blanket and nestling in Milly’s arms as he did his best to figure out this nursing stuff.

As he rooted and snuffled, Milly’s gaze flicked worriedly between her son and Cait. “Am I doing this right?”

“You’re doing fine,” Cait assured her. “Here.” She reached down and, cradling C.J.’s head, helped ease him to a slightly different angle so he could find the nipple.

"Ouch," Milly exclaimed as her son finally glommed on.

"Hey," Cash said with gruff tenderness to the baby, "you're not supposed to hurt your mom." He was sitting next to her on the edge of the bed, and he brushed a lock of hair off her cheek. "He already did hurt you," he said, the memories of Milly's labor obviously still fresh in his mind.

"He was worth it," Milly said fervently. She stroked the baby's soft cheek.

"They're always worth it," Cait said softly as she stood back and watched the new little family group.

She never delivered a baby that she didn't feel a pang of envy for what the parents had and she didn't.

She would, she assured herself. She was young enough yet. Twenty-nine wasn't that old. And both she and Steve wanted children.

Steve Carmichael. Her fiancé. The man she had been waiting for all her life.

They wanted the same things, she and Steve: home, family, children.

Three, she'd said, though Steve wasn't sure about that.

"How on earth will we have time for them?" he asked. "We can't even find time to get married."

He had a point. Steve was a cardiologist, presently practicing in Bozeman, but coming to Livingston two afternoons a week. In August he was taking a new job at a teaching hospital in Denver. Now he spent one week a month there getting established, making the transition.

Cait had demands on her time, as well. She was a nurse-midwife who not only worked with two physicians, but delivered babies, like C.J., on her own. She taught childbirth classes one night a week. And since her father's heart attack had brought her home late last summer, she'd been in charge of running the family ranch.

She'd expected her father to be back at it by now, but his recovery had been slower than anticipated. Always a vital, active man, Walt Blasingame now sat and stared out the window for hours. He had no energy, no enthusiasm. Cait tried to encourage him, run the ranch, and do her job. And, even though she'd hired a foreman this spring, she still didn't have much time for thinking about a wedding.

"Never mind," Steve said. "We'll get to it. I can always come back from Denver for a wedding. What matters is that we've found each other."

Amen to that, Cait thought. At last she had found the right man to marry.

Steve was solid, dependable, committed. He wanted exactly what she wanted—a refreshing change from the man she'd first set her heart on.

She barely spared him a thought anymore. Since she'd met Steve she had settled, relaxed, got her bearings once more. At last she felt as if her feet were on emotionally steady ground.

If there was a silver lining to the cloud that had been her father's heart attack, it was her coming home and finding Steve.

He thought so, too. "We're perfect together. We understand each other."

Only another medical professional could appreciate the emergencies, the unforeseen events that complicated life on a weekly and sometimes almost daily basis. Steve called and canceled dates because of someone's heart attack. She called and canceled dates because of someone's birth.

When they could, they enjoyed the time they had.

And when they finally had a family, Cait knew they would make things work.

She wouldn't have the ranch to worry about then. Either her father would be back running things or her brother,

Wes, would finally decide it was time to come home and do it, or—and she didn't like to think about this—the Rafter WB would be sold.

It wouldn't matter to her, she told herself. She'd be in Denver, anyway.

But the ranch was so much a part of her that she couldn't imagine it not being there to come home to.

It always had been.

She'd gone all over the world in the past seven years. She'd started at a prenatal clinic in Mexico. She had ended up staying to work as a nurse through one of the most devastating earthquakes to hit the region. After that, going back to Livingston to work had seemed almost a cop-out. There were so many other people and places who urgently needed medical aid.

If she, footloose and fancy-free, couldn't help out, who would?

So she'd spent the next seven years going from one disaster to another. Not just natural disasters, either. Some of them were man-made. Wars, to put it bluntly. Someone had to help. It might as well be her.

But in the back of her mind she'd always carried the ranch with her. She'd taken it out and talked about it, shared it with others, given them a taste of her home.

Once she'd dreamed about bringing them home.

One man.

One child.

She wouldn't let herself think about the man anymore.

She still thought about the child.

Resi.

The thought of the little orphaned girl who had wormed her way into Cait's heart made her throat tighten and an ache begin behind her eyes.

"Stop it!" she told herself sharply aloud. It wasn't productive, thinking about Resi. It wasn't even smart. There was nothing to be sad about. Everything had turned out for the best. Everything!

Cait had stopped counting the times she had assured herself of that.

The memories came back when she was tired, when she was vulnerable, when she saw families like the Callahans and knew how fortunate they were.

Now she finished washing up, dragged a brush through her hair and grabbed her tote bag. It was nine-thirty. She'd put in a full day before delivering C.J., and she still had to drive thirty odd miles and check with Gus Holt, the foreman, about how things were going at the ranch. But first she was going to see how the new family was doing.

The baby was sleeping in Milly's arms. Milly herself was dozing. Cash was sitting in the armchair by the bed, a stunned but blissful expression on his face. When Cait came into the room he looked up and grinned.

"I can't hardly catch my breath," he said, then gave a self-deprecating laugh. "I've seen calves born before. I know my birds an' bees. But that was a miracle tonight." He shook his head in amazement.

"It always is." Cait went over to the bed, and Milly opened her eyes to smile up at her. "You doing all right?"

Milly nodded. "Fine. Just fine." Her voice was a whisper. She brushed a gentle finger over C.J.'s soft hair. "Isn't he something?"

"He's something," Cait agreed. "Can I do anything else for you before I leave?"

Milly shook her head. "You've already done everything."

"Well, give me a call if you need anything. I'll be in tomorrow morning to check on you. The doctor will be by, too, just to check things out. You rest now. The nurse can put C.J. in the isolette for you." She nodded toward the one that had been wheeled into the room so C.J. and his mother wouldn't be separated. "You look like you could use some sleep, too," she said to Cash, who was still smiling his dazed, delighted grin.

"Go home and go to sleep now," Milly said to him.

Cash looked as if he was going to protest, but he didn't. "Yes, ma'am," he said. Then he bent down and dropped a light kiss on his son's head and another deeper more intense one on his wife's mouth. "God, Mil', I do love you," he said.

Cait, watching them, felt another stab of envy and swallowed the lump in her throat.

Someday, she promised herself, as she led the way and Cash followed her out, that would be her in the birthing suite. And it would be Steve kissing her and telling her he loved her and looking at her like that, with his heart in his eyes.

She and Cash walked toward the lobby together. When they reached it, he put his arm around her and gave her a hard hug. "God, Cait, I don't know how to thank you. I am the happiest, luckiest guy in the world."

Cait smiled. "Tonight, Cash," she said, "I'd have to agree with you. Just remember it a week from now when he's crying at 2:00 a.m."

He grinned and crossed his heart. "I promise."

They started toward the door when Joyce O'Meara, the receptionist, called, "Cait?"

"Go on," she said to Cash. "I'll see you tomorrow."

"Right. G'night. Thank you." He sketched her a quick salute, gave her a wink and sauntered out into the night.

"What is it?" she asked.

Joyce nodded toward the shadowy waiting room. "There's someone waiting to see you."

Please God, not someone in labor, Cait thought wearily. Smiling, she turned—and felt the bottom fall out of her world.

A lean dark man had hauled himself awkwardly out of a chair and stepped out of the shadows. The light fell on his blue-black hair and sharp, handsome, weather-beaten face.

"Charlie?"

Oh, God, no.

But it was. Charlie Seeks Elk in the flesh, right here, big as life, smiling that beautiful lopsided smile of his. "Hello, Cait."

Two

He didn't know what to say.

He'd driven all the way from California, had rehearsed his greeting at least a thousand times. And now, when he finally came face-to-face with her, the words stuck in his throat.

He just wanted to reach out to her, to put his arms around her and hang on. No one in his entire life had ever looked so good.

And so shocked.

And not exactly thrilled.

Charlie could read visuals better than most. It was, after all, what he did for a living. And he could read this visual with no problem at all.

Cait wasn't glad to see him. She looked, in fact, gut-punched.

She wetted her lips, but she didn't smile. She said his name again. "Charlie." Her fingers, one hand free, one hand clutching a tote bag, balled into fists.

He felt the first flicker of true apprehension since he'd fought his way back from eternity all those months ago. And he tried again. "I don't suppose you'd believe I was just in the neighborhood?"

"I don't suppose I would," she said coolly. She didn't look gut-punched now. The color in her cheeks, which had drained briefly, was coming back. She looked flushed and fit and absolutely wonderful.

"I wasn't," he said. "I came to see you."

The balled fist opened, and Cait tucked one hand into her pocket. The other strangled the handle of the tote. "I can't imagine why."

He didn't suppose she could. He took a deep breath and it was his turn to wet suddenly parched lips. He could feel a pulsing throb in his still-healing leg. It wasn't as steady as he would have wished. *He* wasn't as steady.

He rubbed a hand against taut muscles at the back of his neck. "Could we...go somewhere and talk?"

"What could we possibly have to say to each other?"

It was going to be harder than he thought. He shouldn't have been surprised, after all. And really, he wasn't. He hadn't been expecting a miracle. He'd had no illusions that she would take one look and throw her arms around him. He wasn't exactly the prodigal son.

He was the man who had left her without a word, had walked out in the middle of the night and had never come back—until now.

"I have some things to say," he said slowly and more steadily than he felt, "even if you don't. I wish you'd listen."

"Why should I?"

He looked straight at her. "I don't know."

Something flickered in her stubborn, unblinking gaze. Some tiny movement seemed to make her hesitate. She bit down on her lip and glanced around.

The receptionist was listening avidly and with no pretense about it. Charlie didn't care.

Obviously Cait did. One look at the woman's eager expression and Cait's lips pressed into a tight line. "Fine," she said curtly. "You can talk. There's a fast-food place not far from here. We can meet there for a cup of coffee."

She turned on her heel and headed for the door.

For a split second Charlie just watched her, drank in the sight of her—even the stiff, unyielding back of her. Then he strode after her, trying not to limp, aware of the receptionist's curious gaze.

Cait was waiting outside, keys in her hand. "You do have a car?" She barely looked back at him as she spoke.

He nodded. "Over there."

She didn't even glance where he had pointed. "That's my truck." She indicated an older full-size red Ford. "Follow me." She turned and started briskly away.

"Cait!"

She turned. "What?" Truck keys tapped impatiently against her thigh.

"I need—" He broke off. He couldn't explain. There were no explanations. Just need. A need that had been roiling desperately inside him since he'd looked around his eternity and discovered she wasn't there.

"What?" she said irritably.

He shouldn't. It was probably only going to make things worse. But he couldn't help it. Couldn't stop himself.

"Need this," he finished, and closed the gap between them, wrapped his arms around her and laid his lips on hers.

He was kissing Cait. Hungrily. Desperately. Like a drowning man opening to the gasp of air before he's swept away. He was holding Cait. He was knowing once more what it was like to have her in his arms, to wrap them around her, to fit her body to his, to mold them into one.

But her body wasn't fitting. It wasn't molding. She stood rigid and unbending, her arms stiff at her sides, her lips tightly shut.

Oh, hell. Oh, hell. Oh, hell.

And then, just as he was about to give up, he felt something—a softening, a warming—a kindling that was happening in spite of her determination that it should not. He could feel it.

And he thought, *Yes!*

And he dared to believe at last that things would be all right. She still cared. She loved him. She would take him back.

And then, abruptly, Cait pulled away from him. Her eyes were fierce and angry and brimming with pain.

"Ah, Cait," he said, still heartened in spite of the pain he saw there, certain he could heal it with the right words. "I didn't meant to hurt you."

She didn't move, barely even opened her lips. "Do you want that cup of coffee or not?"

Her voice was hard and clipped, but he believed. More, he could still taste just a hint of her, was still close enough that the scent of her—a scent that had always made even the worst of Abuk's nightmares go away—touched his nostrils.

How the hell had he ever managed to walk away from her?

How could he explain what he had done?

"I want the cup of coffee," he said. His throat ached.

"Then follow me." Her voice was cool, steady, at odds with the pain he'd seen in her eyes. She turned and walked ramrod straight to her truck.

She was shaking so badly that it took her three tries to get the key in the ignition. She finally got it when she grabbed her right hand in her left to steady it and jammed the key in and turned it on.

Then she gripped the steering wheel with both trembling hands and took deep, deep breaths.

Charlie! Here!

And even worse, kissing her!

Thank God she'd steeled herself the moment he'd taken her into his arms.

It hadn't been easy. He felt the same—hard and lean and warm. Maybe even a little harder and leaner than she remembered. He smelled the same. There was that hint of lime and leather and something indefinably Charlie.

The memories had swamped her, made her ache and need—and want things she knew she absolutely did not want at all.

She was done with him—just as he had been done with her.

When she'd awakened that morning in Abuk to find herself alone in bed, she'd simply assumed that Charlie had got a call that had taken him out on an early lead and she hadn't heard it. She worked twelve-hour days in conditions that no one should have to work in—and when she slept, she slept like a rock. She rarely heard Charlie's phone.

She hadn't been surprised to find him gone.

It had happened before. When you did what Charlie did for a living, you never knew when something would happen.

Something *had* happened.

She didn't realize until later that what had happened was that Charlie had walked out of her life.

Why?

She'd screamed the question. She'd cried it. She'd asked it a hundred times. And yet, if she opened herself to the silence, she already knew.

He hadn't loved her.

It was as simple and as stark as that.

She'd been fine to have an affair with, had been right there, ready and available for a desperate, passionate fling, the sort one had in the middle of a war zone where no one looked beyond today because tomorrow might never come.

The problem was that the night before Charlie had walked, Cait had dared to talk about tomorrow.

She had talked about *all* their tomorrows. She had talked about forever. Marriage. Family.

And when she'd awakened, he was gone.

And now, two years later, he was here...and he wanted to talk.

Cait didn't want to talk. She didn't want to listen.

Most of all, she didn't want to feel what she'd felt when he'd kissed her.

Damn him! It was over. Completely over!

And she was over him!

She had a new man now. A better man.

And she was going to tell him so.

She wished they had just "talked" in the hospital waiting room. She didn't want to drag this out any longer than necessary. But it was probably better, she thought, closing her eyes and praying for strength, that they did it somewhere else.

If they'd stayed at the hospital, Joyce would have heard every word.

Joyce was a good soul, but she knew Cait and she knew Steve—and a strange man and Cait Blasingame having a heart-to-heart in the hospital waiting room would give her lots of fodder for the gossip mill.

There would be plenty to talk about, anyway, simply because Charlie had showed up looking for her. And if Joyce had happened to glance outside and see that kiss...!

Cait didn't even want to think about that.

In her rearview mirror she saw a low-slung sports car—good God, was he driving a Porsche?—pull out of a stall, then come to idle close by. She could see Charlie behind the wheel, watching her, waiting for her.

"Do it," she told herself firmly. "You can do this. Talk to him. Walk away from him."

How hard could it be? It couldn't possibly be worse than being left in the middle of the night?

There were several fast-food joints not far from the hospital. She picked one where she hoped she wouldn't know anyone and parked just outside the door. She got out and waited as Charlie's car—it was, in fact, a silver Porsche!—glided to a stop alongside hers. Her fingers clenched involuntarily, and she consciously unfolded them and brushed them down the sides of her slacks.

The car door opened and Charlie got out. He moved as if he hurt. Cait looked away. She wouldn't ask. She didn't care. Her fingers curled tightly again.

"You look good," he said in that rough-silk voice of his as he came up to her.

"You don't," she said bluntly, making a point at looking him over now.

The light in the hospital had been soft, and it hadn't shown the new lines and hollows in his lean, gaunt face. They told her that the past two years had been hard ones. She knew about some of it—she'd seen the photos in his book.

Fool that she was, she'd bought it.

Resi, after all, was on the cover. She'd bought it because of Resi—because she had been a part of the poignant story of the life that Charlie had told in pictures.

That was the only reason. But of course she'd looked at it all. After he'd left Abuk she learned that he had gone to Africa, into an area that was, if possible, even more ravaged. The life his photos showed there had been much the same. Obviously, it had had its effects on him, too.

He was smiling at her now, but she noticed that it didn't reach his eyes. They were dark and serious.

"No," he said now, in reply to her blunt assessment of his looks, "I don't suppose I do." He held the door open, and she went in.

If Cait had ever let herself imagine seeing Charlie Seeks Elk again, it wouldn't have been beneath the glaring lights of a fast-food restaurant in Livingston, Montana, on a warm breezy summer night.

Charlie had never been inclined to come to Montana. He'd even teased her about her "country girl" life, though sometimes she thought he might actually have envied it just a little.

When she'd first met him she'd assumed he was, like many Indians she knew, born on a reservation from which he'd left to find a place in the world beyond it. He hadn't been, he'd told her.

"The L.A. kid, that's me. Born and bred." He'd gone on to tell her in a few brief, stark sentences about his childhood. His father had been born on a reservation, though Charlie didn't even know which tribe it belonged to. He'd left to join the army and, after his discharge, he'd stayed in L.A.

"What'd he have to go back to?" Charlie had said with a shrug. "Nothing for him there. Besides, he drank. He could drink anywhere."

He'd met Charlie's mother in L.A. where she worked as a secretary. "My mom's family were dust-bowl Okies, mostly Choctaw, on the rolls at least," he'd said. "But they left in the thirties. No future for them there."

They hadn't had much of a future in any case.

Charlie's parents had had barely eight years together before his father's drinking led him to have a fatal car accident. Charlie had been three, his sister, Lucy, eight. Their mother had worked hard. She'd done her best for them. In fact, she'd been so focused on providing for them that she had neglected her own health and missed the warning signs of diabetes until it was too late.

She'd died when Charlie was eleven. Lucy, at sixteen, decided she was old enough to take charge.

"Luce did her best," Charlie had told Cait late one night. They were lying in bed, listening to gunfire, and it was the only time he'd ever talked about his sister. "She just didn't know how hard it was going to be. She wouldn't get help, wouldn't ask. She was afraid they'd take me away from her." He'd lain silent for a long time, looking at the wall, not at Cait. The gunfire rattled on, and Charlie said tonelessly, "She got herself killed on the streets."

Cait looked at him now, remembering all that, resisting the memory.

Charlie was ordering two cups of coffee.

"Do you want anything else?" he asked. She shook her head. "One with milk," he told the spotty boy behind the counter.

She was surprised that he remembered how she took her coffee. She wished he hadn't.

While he was paying, she turned away and found a table on the far side of the room, grateful that she didn't know any of the few other patrons and didn't have to introduce him to anyone. Taking the bench seat, she slid in. She could see the room then. She could be the one who would sit protected with the wall at her back.

As if he understood, Charlie was smiling a little wryly as he came toward her. Unless she closed her eyes or deliberately looked away, Cait had to watch him cross the room.

He didn't move the way he used to. Charlie had always had a smooth, easy gait that had reminded her of a mountain lion on the prowl. He'd always been quick and lithe. "You move like a cat," she'd said once.

"An alley cat," Charlie had agreed.

Now his movements were much less graceful. He moved slowly and carefully, and there was a hesitation in his gait. Cait was certain that his caution owed less to the fact that he was carrying two full cups of coffee than that he had tangled with something bigger and stronger and tougher sometime in the past two years.

When he reached the table, he set one cup, a stirrer and three small half-and-half containers in front of her, then put his own down and took the seat opposite her. She saw him wince a little as he bent his leg to sit down.

"What happened?" She couldn't not ask, but she was glad her voice sounded cool and mostly indifferent when she did.

"I got shot."

It struck her as odd the way he said it. It wasn't offhand exactly, but the old Charlie would have made a joke of it.

"The bastards tried to blow me away," he would have said, and then he would have laughed at just one more brush with death.

But this Charlie wasn't laughing.

He peeled the top off his cup of coffee and sat with his hands wrapped around it. His fingers were laced together and his knuckles looked almost white with strain. Cait stared at them, then lifted her gaze to his eyes once more.

He closed his eyes for just a second and, with his fingers knit together like that, he almost looked as if he was praying.

Saying grace over a coffee cup? Cait thought. Charlie? Hardly.

Then he opened them again and took a breath. "That's why I'm here." His fingers clenched just a fraction. "Because I got shot." Another breath. His hands shifted a little on the cup. "Because I almost died. Actually—" that wry corner of his mouth lifted again "—I did die. Coded, I think the word is. I saw eternity." He stopped, but his eyes never left her face. "And you weren't there."

A group of teenagers across the room were laughing and arguing. The milk shake machine was whirring madly. There was the faint sound of the electronic voice from the drive-up saying something about taking an order, please.

And Charlie was talking about getting shot and dying and seeing eternity and her...*what?* Not being there?

Cait felt as if the world was spinning. The roar in her brain was deafening. She just stared. The pit of her stomach burned and she hadn't even yet drunk the coffee.

She wondered eventually if he expected a response. She couldn't imagine what one would be.

But apparently he didn't expect one, because after a moment's silence he went on. "I couldn't face eternity without you, so I came back."

"To life?" The words, thank God, came automatically and sarcastically and not without a certain measure of self-defensiveness.

But Charlie simply nodded. "Yes."

Cait shook her head. She reached for one of the half-and-half containers and, with trembling fingers, ripped the top off and dumped the contents into her cup. Then she did the same with the second and with the last. It was too much milk. She liked two, not three. She didn't care. She had to do something—and that was the only thing there was.

Agitated, she stirred the coffee. She didn't look at Charlie. But she could feel his eyes on her. Scrutinizing.

All of a sudden she was furiously angry. How dare he!

"Let me get this straight," she said finally, as evenly as she could. "You got shot. You died. And when you got to heaven or hell or wherever you went, I wasn't there so you came back?'' She was looking at him now. Her eyes were shooting daggers at him.

He didn't flinch. He looked, if anything, calmer. ''More or less. Yes. Of course, I didn't think I'd died. I knew I'd been shot. I got caught in a crossfire. Hit three times. I lost a lot of blood. I could hear them taking me to the hospital. Tony Sellers and another guy. I could hear them yelling at each other, and they must have finally got me to the hospital because all of a sudden it sounded less like streets and more like buildings. Gurneys. Metal. You know?''

He didn't wait for her reply but went on. ''And that's when I started seeing this light. It was really bright, like sunlight at the end of a tunnel. And then it started spreading out, like when the sun comes up, spilling light all over, and I began to see people.'' His eyes came back to meet hers for just a second.

Then they drifted away again and he was staring off into the middle distance. ''I saw my father,'' he said quietly, ''and my mother. And my sister.''

''Who are all dead,'' Cait said impatiently. He had told her once that he was the only one left in his whole family.

''And then I saw Chase and Joanna and their kids. And the Cavanaughs and the Craigs. You remember me talking about them?''

She nodded reluctantly. They were friends of the Whitelaws and, barring a total disaster, she was sure they weren't all dead.

''And my buddies from high school, Lopez and DeShayne.'' Charlie smiled faintly. ''I even saw goofy old Herbert who could spit water through his front teeth. I saw a lot of other people.'' He paused and studied the tabletop for a long moment, then looked up once more. ''But I didn't see you.''

''Maybe I didn't get an invitation,'' Cait said tartly.

''You didn't.''

"Well, then..."

"Because I'd walked out on you."

"Tell me something I don't know."

"I love you."

Oh, God, no! Please, not that! Don't let him say that.

Cait's feet thumped, firm and flat on the floor, bracing her. She clutched the coffee cup so tightly that she was in danger of crushing it and sending coffee all over the table. "Don't," she said fiercely through her teeth. "Tell. Me. That."

"It's true."

"And that's why you left in the middle of the night?"

Charlie shook his head and raked a hand through his hair. "I didn't know it then. I didn't *want* to know it then," he corrected himself.

"How nice for you," Cait said bitterly. "Well, how about this—I don't want to know it now."

She tried to shove her chair back, realized she was sitting against the wall and couldn't shove anywhere. So, clumsily, she slid out the side of the bench and got to her feet. "I'm going home."

Charlie hauled himself awkwardly to his feet, too. "Cait, don't. Finish your coffee. Talk to me. God, I know it's weird. But it's true."

"It might be true, that doesn't matter. I don't have to listen to it!" She started toward the door.

He followed her, dogged her footsteps. "Look, Cait. I know I hurt you. Bad. I know that. I was wrong. I'm sorry."

She kept right on walking, head high, facing straight ahead. Not until she had gone out the door and reached her dad's old truck did she stop and turn to confront him. "Yes, well, I'm sorry, too. But that is over. It's finished. It's been *two years,* Charlie!"

"That's not a long time compared to eternity." His voice was quiet. Steady. Reasonable.

All the things she was not.

Cait folded her arms tightly across her breasts and shivered, anyway, feeling the cool night air knife down the back of her neck. She didn't want to turn and look at him, but she knew she had to, knew he wouldn't settle for less. So she turned. She stared straight into his eyes.

The best defense was a good offense. Wes had always taught her that.

"So what now, Charlie? Why are you here? What do you want?"

He seemed to balance lightly, not awkward at all now. Settled, cool. Like a gunfighter, she thought. Like a man in control.

"I want you to marry me, Cait."

She'd had to ask.

All the bright and shining dreams she'd once had—of the future, of the two of them, of a lifetime and an eternity spent together—rose up once more.

Ruthlessly she crushed them right back down.

"I'm already getting married, Charlie—to someone else."

A semi rumbled past above on the Interstate. The teenagers, still talking and laughing, jostled their way out of the restaurant and tumbled into a pair of pickup trucks and roared away.

He didn't move. He opened his mouth, but for a long moment no sound came out. Then at last he said, "You can't."

Red flashed before her eyes. "What do you mean, *I can't?* Who the hell are you to tell me what I can and can't do?"

He took a ragged breath. "I mean…you kissed me. You—"

"*You* kissed me, Charlie!"

"You responded!"

"No, I didn't!"

But damn it, yes, for just an instant she had. She crushed that thought, too. She hugged herself tighter.

"No, I didn't," she repeated with all the quiet force she could muster.

He just looked at her. "Cait." He said her name gently, cajolingly, persuasively.

She steeled herself against him. "No. I'm sorry you almost got killed, Charlie. I'm sorry you nearly died. I appreciate the fact that you 'missed' me in 'eternity.' But I'm marrying someone else."

"Who?"

"What difference does it make? You don't know him."

"Do you?"

"How dare you? How dare you come back into my life after two years and just assume that I'm going to jump into your arms? You hurt me, Charlie! You walked out! You left me cold and you never even said why! I *know* why. I'm not stupid. I figured it out. You didn't want anything more than an affair. You didn't want marriage. You didn't want a family. You didn't want what I wanted. You didn't love me."

"I—"

"You didn't love me," she repeated. She would *not* allow him to deny that! "And it hurt. I got past it, though. I'm over it. I have a life. I have a job. I have a fiancé. His name is Steve. He's a cardiologist. And yes, I know him. I also love him! And he's worth ten of you."

He didn't say a word. He let her wind down. And a smart thing for him, too, or she'd have steamrolled right over him.

"He probably is," Charlie said quietly. "But I love you.

And you love me, too. If you didn't—'' he rode right over her protest ''—you wouldn't have responded at all.''

''I can't help what you read into things, Charlie. You hear what you want to hear. You see what you want to see and nothing else. You always have.''

Her arrow hit home. She saw something flicker in his gaze. A muscle ticked in his jaw.

''I love you,'' he repeated. ''I was wrong to leave you. I was a fool.'' He still sounded calm, but the calm was edged with urgency now. His stare was intent. ''Don't compound it, Cait. Don't make the same mistake I did.''

''The only mistake I made, Charlie,'' she said with all the bravado she could muster, ''was two years ago, when I fell in love with you.''

''So,'' Gaby's voice trilled in his ear as he lay on the motel room bed staring at the ceiling. ''When's the wedding?''

''Very funny.'' His voice sounded raw even to his ears.

''Oh.'' Her tone changed at once. ''You talked to her?''

''Yes, I talked to her. And no, she doesn't want to marry me. She's marrying someone else.''

''Who?''

''Some guy named Steve. Some cardiologist. And now you know everything I know,'' Charlie said, still angry. ''So why don't you just drop it?''

There was a moment's pause. Then, ''Are you going to drop it?''

Charlie stared at the ceiling a long moment, seeing Cait with her arms tightly folded across her breasts, defending herself against him—or against herself? He hadn't imagined that momentary response. He was sure he hadn't. He knew Cait. He knew her body, the way it reacted, the way it loved.

But could he convince her?

Did he have any right to try?

Yes, of course he did. If she still loved him, she shouldn't be marrying someone else! It would be wrong-headed and downright dumb. She had to see that.

"No," he said at last. "No, I'm not dropping it."

It hadn't been easy to walk away from Cait the first time. He'd wanted to stay, but he'd been afraid of the commitment. Now he wasn't. Now he welcomed it.

He wasn't going to walk away a second time.

Not as long as he had any hope at all.

And he did have hope. For all that she'd denied still loving him, she still felt something—even if only for an instant.

Charlie was a photographer. He had built his life on moments caught in the blink of a shutter. That was what he'd felt in Cait's response.

He was willing to work with that.

"You said something about a cabin," he said to Gaby. "Some friend of yours?"

"Brenna McCall."

"Right. Would she rent it to me?"

"Are we talking a long siege here?"

"I don't know what we're talking. Will she rent it?"

"I can call her and ask. She offered it for a few nights already, if you recall."

Charlie hadn't been thinking about that then. He'd only been thinking about getting to Cait. Then he'd thought in the short term. Not now.

"I'd appreciate it," he said.

"Do you want me to tell her why? The *real* reason why," Gaby said, "or do you want me to blather on about you needing a place to regroup and take some pretty pictures? She knows you know Cait, but I didn't go into details."

"Let's keep it that way," Charlie said.

If she was engaged, he needed to move carefully. He didn't want to cause her embarrassment or pain. He simply wanted her back.

"Just tell her I want a change of pace. Tell her I'm working on my new vision."

Gaby chuckled. "What vision would that be?"

"I don't know. I'll tell you when I find it."

"I'll give her your phone number at the motel. I don't think it will be a problem. She won't be using the cabin herself for a while. She and Jed had another baby this spring, so she won't be going off to paint for a while. If you don't hear from her by tomorrow night, call me back."

"Will do. And, Gaby, thanks."

"Oh, I do this all the time for my clients, Charlie." She laughed. "I'll just be expecting you to name one of the girls after me."

One of the girls. Kids with Cait.

Scary thoughts. Notions that had sent him packing two years ago.

And now—Charlie stared at the ceiling some more—his dearest wish.

"Dr. Carmichael," the muttered voice was clearly sleep-fogged, and Cait felt immediately guilty for having called him so late.

"I'm sorry, Steve. I didn't realize what time it was." Now she looked at the clock and discovered it was almost two in the morning. "I'll let you go back to sleep."

"No. Don't hang up." He cleared his throat, yawned, then said, "What's up? Bad night?"

Sometimes they called each other when things were rough—when he lost a patient he was sure he'd be able to save, when she had a delivery that went wrong.

"No," Cait said hastily, because it wasn't—not like that, anyway. "I just...got lonesome."

Panic-stricken, more like. She'd trembled all the way home after her confrontation with Charlie. She'd taken deep breaths and tried to steady her racing pulse. She'd strangled the steering wheel trying to get an emotional grip.

It was the shock, she'd told herself. Seeing him would have been enough to set off heart palpitations. A proposal of marriage was the last thing she expected.

Or wanted.

She didn't need that! She didn't need him!

And so when she got home, she'd paced furiously, then she'd taken a long shower, hoping she'd be able to wash away the memories and the jumble of thoughts chasing each other through her mind.

But nothing had worked. Nothing had calmed her.

Nothing would, she realized, until she talked to Steve.

She needed to connect to the real man in her life, not the one who had just burst back onto the scene. Now she curled up in the armchair, tucked her robe around her and let the soft sleepy sound of Steve breathing settle her jangled nerves.

There was another yawn from Steve's end of the line. She heard him stretch. "Well, good." There was a hint of a smile in his still-sleepy voice. "I always like to talk to you. Even in the middle of the night. Is your dad okay?"

"Dad's okay. I'm just lonesome. Cash and Milly Callahan had their baby tonight."

"Ah." Steve smiled. "The hormones are responding."

"Maybe. Yes. That must be it." Better to think that than to think about Charlie.

She wondered if she should tell Steve about Charlie, then decided not to.

No man wanted to be awakened and told that his fiancée couldn't sleep because she couldn't stop thinking about the man she used to be in love with.

"Want to meet for breakfast?" he asked her. "I'm going to be in Livingston tomorrow. I don't have any appointments here in the morning. I could come over early. We could grab one of those egg and muffin things."

"I don't think so." There was no way she was going back to the place she'd just been with Charlie! "I have appointments in the morning. But how about tomorrow night? We could catch a movie?"

"If your beeper doesn't go off." She could hear the smile in his voice.

"Or if yours doesn't."

They chuckled together. Yes, Cait thought, hugging the notion to herself, they were definitely compatible.

"Okay. Movie it is." Steve yawned again. "Anything else?"

Just keep talking to me, Cait wanted to say. But she couldn't make Steve stay awake all night just to stop her thinking about Charlie.

"No. I'm all right."

"You sure? Want me to come over?"

Cait laughed. It was a good sixty miles from Steve's place to hers. "No. It's okay. I just...thanks."

"Anytime," he promised. "See you tomorrow night. I'll call you."

"Yes," Cait said. "Please."

"G'night. Dream of me."

"Yes."

But she didn't. She dreamed of Charlie.

Three

Charlie got the cabin. He went up the next day with Brenna leading the way. They'd lent him her father, Otis's, old Suburban. It did gravel and dirt better than Charlie's car.

"You're sure you don't mind?" Charlie had asked.

"Oh, I think we'll manage," Jed had said with a sly smile in the direction of the Porsche.

They probably would. Charlie wasn't sure about himself.

Brenna had come up on horseback, bringing a mount she'd said he could pasture here and use in the hills. He hadn't been sure about that, but she'd insisted.

"You won't want to walk everywhere. Babe is easy. You'll like her."

She showed him how the generator worked. She pointed out the firewood pile in case he wanted a little warmth in the cool summer evenings. Then she stood on the porch, breathed deeply and said, "You'll love it here. Whatever you're looking for, you'll find it."

Charlie hoped she was right.

He dug in, barracked down, and told himself that just being in the vicinity was a start, that while he was here he'd think of a game plan, a way to convince Cait to fall into his arms.

He had no idea what he was getting himself into.

If Montana was the "last best place"—as many of its natives, its literature and its advertising campaigns would have you believe—it was also, in Charlie's mind, the strangest.

When Brenna left him, he was alone. Totally alone. He didn't think he'd ever been alone before in his life.

The sheer silence was unnerving.

Weird, he thought. Very very weird.

He walked around the cabin, admired the view across the Shields Valley toward what Brenna told him were the Crazy Mountains.

"Crazy?"

"They say an old woman went crazy from loneliness up there," she'd told him.

As afternoon turned into evening and evening into night and he still didn't see anyone else or hear anyone else, Charlie began to understand what she meant.

He had a hard time falling asleep that night. It was too quiet. He had too much time to think.

That's what he told himself.

But then he started thinking about Cait and remembering the stories she'd told about her home. He was here now.

He could hear the horse whickering. Some cows were lowing. There was an odd soft rushing sound he didn't recognize. It took him a while but he finally worked out what it was—the wind soughing through the pine trees.

He was here. In Cait's state. In the land she called home.

He didn't awaken until midday.

He'd never slept so soundly. He'd barely ever slept so long. It was the altitude, he told himself. But he didn't feel tired, he felt energized, curious about this new world he was inhabiting.

The first full day he spent at the cabin, he never saw another person. He never heard another person. He never talked to anyone.

The only things he heard were the whinnies of Babe, the horse, the cawing of a couple of jays, the occasional hoot of something that was probably an owl, the sound of his own footsteps as he moved around the small spartan cabin. And he heard the wind.

Sometimes it was the soft rushing sound he'd heard in the night. Sometimes it shifted and sawed through the trees. He went outside for a walk and heard it whistling through the long grass, saw the stalks bending in the breeze.

He began to hear the wind play an orchestra's worth of nature's instruments and found himself bewitched by every one. It almost seemed to talk to him.

And once he got past the strangeness, he liked hearing what it had to say.

In its whisper, he heard echoes of stories Cait had told of her childhood here. He remembered her talking about lying awake at night in a sleeping bag on the mountainside listening to the wind, and he had tried to imagine it.

Now he didn't have to imagine.

He could hear what she had heard.

The sounds and the memories of Cait's stories, of Cait herself, mingled together and exhilarated him.

They also grounded him—and challenged him. But it wasn't the desperate challenge he'd felt when she'd said she was engaged. It wasn't the frantic need to turn her head and argue with her to make her see she was wrong.

He couldn't make her see.

Like Chase said, he had to get himself balanced, get in harmony with this world in which he found himself, this world to which she belonged. He had to *be*.

Then, God willing, she would see for herself.

The first few days weren't easy. The old Charlie periodically wanted to rev his engine, go down the mountain and bulldoze his way back into Cait's life.

But the longer he stayed, the more he understood that bulldozing was out of place.

He remembered Chase once telling him about the time he'd met his father and had decided to stay on the Navajo reservation.

"It took some getting used to," he'd said with what Charlie imagined was his usual understatement. "But I needed it. I had to do it. I had to find out who I was."

That had surprised Charlie at the time. Chase had seemed pretty well sorted out to him. Now he understood that a man could look sorted out and still have pieces missing.

He'd come to find Cait, but he was starting to find himself, too.

At first Charlie didn't explore much. His leg bothered him every day. It was weak, and the ground was uneven. He saddled Babe and rode her a few times, but the two of them scared off the wildlife. And the longer he was there, the more Charlie wanted to see the animals that Cait had talked about. So he began leaving Babe behind and going out on his own.

He preferred hiking. It was easier to see, to stop, to listen.

This world was completely different from the one he knew. He might as well have been on another planet. Weaned on concrete and broken glass, window bars and concertina wire, Charlie now saw mountain peaks and prairie grasses, frolicking horses and ambling cattle.

He shot photo after photo, feeling like a kid in a candy store.

A lot of them were garden-variety calendar shots. Pretty pictures of the sort that he used to disdain. But where he once looked for despair and pain and inhumanity and, with his camera, trapped it, now he saw more.

His eye found beauty in the opening of a flower, in the soaring of a hawk, in the gathering bank of clouds that presaged a summer storm.

Now that he'd seen the "wilds" of Montana, he found another reason to be grateful he hadn't been killed four months ago—he not only wouldn't have had Cait, he'd have missed all this.

For a week Cait waited for the other shoe to drop.

She came around corners warily, always expecting to see Charlie. She picked up the phone nervously, sure that she would hear him there.

But days turned into a week without a sign of him. One week turned into two and he wasn't anywhere.

Not anywhere here.

She almost felt as if she'd dreamed the whole thing.

"What were you on about?" Steve had asked her. "Calling in the middle of the night like that?"

"You were right. It was just the Callahans' baby. I was thinking. That's all."

"Well, think about setting a wedding date, then," Steve said.

"Yes," Cait agreed. "I'll do that. Maybe this weekend we can—"

But just then Steve's beeper went off.

* * *

Each day Charlie moved a little farther afield. His leg got stronger.

He would always limp, the doctor had told him. But with each hike, his stamina improved, his muscles strengthened, and the next time he went out, he walked farther still.

He had rarely walked anywhere when he was back home. Why would he, when he had his Porsche?

The car had been one of his most fervent youthful dreams. Chase had had a Porsche when Charlie had first met him. It had been stolen and Charlie had found it, then helped Chase steal it back. It was the moment he and Chase had bonded, for real.

After that he'd deliberately patterned his life after Chase's. And when he could afford it, the Porsche was the first thing he bought.

He couldn't understand Chase selling his Porsche after he married Joanna. But just as Chase had moved beyond the Porsche to a more family oriented vehicle, so Charlie began to think for the first time that maybe the Porsche wasn't what he wanted anymore, either.

It certainly didn't do as well on country gravel as Otis's old Suburban.

A red Ford truck had a certain appeal, too.

So did Babe, though he didn't ride her much. He talked to her every night when he went down to the pasture to give her a sugar cube or two.

She was the only one he talked to.

He could have called anyone on his cell phone. He shut it off. If Gaby wanted to call, she could leave a message with Brenna and Jed.

He didn't want to be bothered. He had a new rhythm to his life.

The strangeness he'd found the first day didn't seem so strange a few days later. The quiet didn't even seem so quiet. Nature had sounds and rhythms all its own. It just took a different sort of hearing to pick them up.

Six months ago he'd have been drumming his fingers, itching to be moving, eager to get back to where the action was.

Now he liked this action.

He liked this place.

And even though he didn't see her, didn't talk to her, didn't even pretend to believe she wanted to see or talk to him again, he felt connected to Cait.

It was her stories that ran through his head as he went to sleep at night. Her words, her memories came back to him as he hiked the mountains during the day.

It was as if she was with him, walking beside him, sharing her home.

It was the knowledge that all this beauty was here waiting for her that kept her going, she'd once told him. If she'd thought the whole world was as strife-ridden and anguished as the part she saw every day, she had confessed one night, she couldn't have borne it.

Her memories had given her hope.

They gave him hope now—of a very different kind.

They gave him hope that all was not lost, that her rejection was not permanent, that her hurt could be assuaged and overcome.

She loved *him.*

"Hate to ask you, Caity," her father said, smiling vaguely at her from the armchair by the window. "I know it's your only day off."

"I don't mind," Cait said. "It's a nice break, checking cattle."

"You'll miss it if you go to Denver," her father said.

"When I go to Denver," Cait corrected. But then she admitted what he was getting at. "Yes, I will."

She loved the ranch, loved the rural work each season.

"Maybe you should talk him into stayin' here."

She shook her head. "He wants to go someplace bigger. He wants to teach."

"What do you want, Caity?" Her father's pale-blue eyes watched her curiously.

Cait took a breath. "Him," she said firmly. "I want him."

It was a shock the first time he saw the bears.

Charlie hadn't ever seen a bear outside of a zoo. It was a little daunting to realize there was no barricade between him and the natural world.

It was fascinating, too.

He crouched behind a clump of scrub to watch them. There was a mother and two cubs along the side of the creek. The mother was poking at something. The cubs were watching. Then she waded in. They splashed. She gave them a hard, maternal look.

Charlie smothered a grin. He lifted his camera.

He began to shoot.

At first he didn't understand what he was seeing. Then he did. It was a lesson. How to catch a fish. Charlie shot half a dozen rolls, entranced. His leg throbbed, but he barely noticed.

First one cub, then the other took swipes at the water, splashing. Mother bear demonstrated again. One of the cubs fell in headfirst.

Charlie smothered a laugh.

He shifted, shot, reloaded. And finally got the moment of triumph on film, when one of the cubs came up with a fish about the size of his hand.

Mother bear looked approving, then turned her back and plodded away into the trees. The cubs splashed for a moment longer, then hurried after her.

And Charlie sat back for the first time in over an hour and realized he could barely bend his knee.

He swore and struggled to his feet. It was a hot afternoon, and flies buzzed around him. He swatted at them, but he didn't think about them. He thought about the bears.

He'd got some good shots. He could sense it. The feeling of exhilaration was back. The energy. If he could find them again tomorrow…

Considering the possibilities, he wasn't watching the ground. He didn't notice the loose rock until his foot hit it. His weak leg buckled and he tumbled. Years of quick thinking inspired him to tuck his body and roll, protecting his camera as he fell. He didn't manage to protect himself.

He crashed down the hillside until he hit a clump of brush.

Stunned, Charlie lay there, gathering his wits, tasting blood. Then slowly he hauled himself to a sitting position, breathing hard.

There was blood in his mouth from a split lip. His face was scratched. His shirt was ripped. He was dirty and scraped up, but he didn't think he'd done any serious damage. Thank God.

It suddenly occurred to him how on his own he really was.

Carefully he hauled himself to his feet. His leg buckled, and he grabbed for a handhold on a pine tree to steady himself. Gingerly he tested it again. It hurt. A lot.

He'd have to put ice on it when he got back to the cabin.

Except he didn't have any ice. The tiny generator-run refrigerator didn't have a freezer compartment.

Too bad. But he'd survive. He'd just hurt for a while.

Slowly, carefully, he turned and, watching what he was doing this time, once more started down.

It was when he heard the sound of a small creek that he had a brainstorm. The creeks up here were nothing but snowmelt. Not quite ice but close. He had learned that wading across one the first morning he'd been there.

On that same hike he'd passed another creek where a natural curve had created a water hole on the far side of one of the fence lines. It had looked like a nice place to take a dip, provided you didn't mind feeling like an ice cube. At the time he'd shuddered at the thought.

Now he didn't.

And even though he could see what looked like possible rain clouds gathering off to the west, he headed in that direction.

When he reached the fence, he gritted his teeth and ducked between the strands of barbwire, then laboriously climbed the hill that overlooked the water hole.

A black horse grazed beneath the cottonwoods, and a pile of clothes sat on a nearby rock. As he watched, a sleek dark head surfaced, and a slim naked body emerged from the water.

It wasn't a cowboy.

It was way too curvy for a cowboy.

Way too gorgeous.

Way too female.

Charlie stopped dead and stared at the naked woman coming out of the water toward him.

Then as he realized who it was, his heart caught in his throat.

What sort of sense of humor did God have?

Cait certainly didn't think it was funny when she walked out of the water hole, looked up and saw Charlie Seeks Elk!

She seriously considered plunging straight back in. She didn't because she refused to let Charlie know he had any effect on her.

In fact, she felt as if she had been run over by a truck.

"What are you doing here?" Then, "What happened to you?" she demanded as she got a look at his scratched, battered clothes and face. And all the while she was trying to get to her clothes.

Charlie unfortunately was in the way. He was grinning ear to ear, limping rapidly down the hill toward her, and apparently not even aware that he was bloody and battered.

"Stop that!" Cait snapped. She glared at his grinning face, furious, embarrassed and mostly willing him to turn around so she could go past him to get to where she'd left her clothes.

Of course he didn't.

"You could turn around," she said frostily. "It would be polite."

Charlie let out a half laugh. "Come on, Cait. You know better than that."

She did, unfortunately. So still steaming, she stalked past him, snatched up her shirt and yanked it on, not bothering with her bra.

She would have needed to dry off before putting that on, and she didn't want to expose herself any more than necessary. At least her shirt had long tails and would cover essentials. She should have known better than to come and take a swim. She wasn't a child anymore.

But today was her day off from the clinic, and she'd spent the entire day moving cattle. It made a change from teaching childbirth classes and seeing pregnant mothers and delivering babies, but she had been hot and tired when she'd finished.

Clouds behind the Bridgers looked as if they might bring rain eventually, but that would have been nowhere near as refreshing as a quick, cool dip.

It had been a spur of the moment decision to take a plunge. And obviously a huge mistake.

As soon as she had her shirt on and buttoned, she

stepped into her panties and dragged them on, then wriggled to get them up over her damp hips. All the while she was aware of Charlie watching her.

Once upon a time she'd liked his eyes on her. They'd made her feel desirable and sexy—and loved.

Now they just made her angry.

With her panties and shirt on and her jeans clutched in front of her, Cait felt covered enough to turn and fix him with a hard stare. "What are you doing? Why are you still here?"

Charlie nodded in the direction from which he'd come. "I'm staying at a place over the hill there. I'm renting a cabin from McCalls."

Cait didn't like the sound of that. "Why?"

"Well, I started because you're here."

She gaped. "You're *spying* on me?"

"Of course not. This was—" he grinned lopsidedly "—pure luck. I had to stay somewhere, didn't I?"

No, he didn't. He should have been long gone.

But before she could say so, he continued, "And Gaby knows Brenna. It's also for my work."

"Is there a war going on in Montana I haven't heard about?" she said sarcastically. From the look of him it seemed possible.

"You mean besides ours?"

"We don't have a war, Charlie. We don't have anything."

"We have a past."

"Exactly."

"And I want us to have a future."

"No."

"I'm not going to pressure you."

Oh, right. "Then what the hell are you doing here? And don't give me that crap about your work. You shoot wars, tragedies, devastation, pain."

"I'm not doin' that anymore."

"What are you doing? Sunsets? Wildflowers? Snow-capped mountain peaks?" she asked flippantly. Charlie had had no use for those kinds of photos when she'd known him.

But he didn't take offense. He said quite seriously. "I wasn't exactly sure, but I think today I might have hit on something. I got some good bears."

Cait stared. "Bears?"

"There were bears up by the creek. A mother and two cubs. She was teaching 'em how to fish."

She wouldn't have believed it if she hadn't seen it, but the look on Charlie's face at the memory of the bears was very like the eagerness he'd shown two years ago faced with a far different scene.

"And they attacked you?" she asked dryly.

He glanced down, almost surprised, as if his clothes belonged to someone else. "Not quite." He shrugged as if it didn't matter. "I fell." His grin quirked for a moment, then, as his gaze dropped and she saw him staring at her legs, the grin faded. He said abruptly, "Do you suppose you could put on those jeans?"

Could she put on her jeans?

As if she'd been standing here trying to seduce him by flaunting her nakedness! Cait felt as if she was burning up!

"By all means," she said through clenched teeth. But she made no move to do so, continuing to glare at him, waiting, until finally he got the point and, giving a negligent shrug, turned around.

Fortunately, the breeze had dried her legs a bit, making it easier for her to stuff first one and then the other into her jeans, which she then dragged up, zipped and snapped.

"There." She glared at his back until he turned around.

"I'm just a little susceptible," Charlie said, not at all repentant. "You remember."

Cait gritted her teeth because, damn it, she did remember. And she didn't want to. It was all too easy to remember when they had been able to heat each other's blood with a mere glance. "Well, I certainly don't want to provide any temptation."

Charlie's smile was rueful. "You don't have to try."

Cait felt her entire body warm under his gaze. "You should put something on that lip," she said gruffly.

Charlie dabbed vaguely at his mouth. "I will. It's why I came here. And I was going to soak my leg." He nodded toward the one he'd been favoring as he'd limped down the hill.

"Did you hurt it?" It was the nurse in her asking. She certainly wasn't asking because she cared.

"Maybe when I fell. It's not a big deal. But the doc always said to put ice on it. And I don't have any ice. But I remembered the water hole."

"I'll leave you to it, then." She bent to snag her boots and socks, then started toward her horse, relieved at the reprieve.

But before she'd got ten feet he called her name. "Cait!"

Reluctantly she turned back. "What?"

"Stay."

And watch him take off his jeans and soak his leg?

"Can't. I've got things to do," she said hastily.

He cocked his head, smiling at her. "You're afraid."

She was surprised there wasn't steam coming out of her ears. "Afraid? Of what?"

"Realizing you still love me…want me." The words were said softly, but the challenge was clearly there.

"If you're implying I can't resist your manly body, you are so wrong."

"Prove it."

Cait lifted her chin and said recklessly, "All right. I will.

Go ahead. Undress. Take your jeans off in front of me. See if I care.''

Slowly Charlie's hands went to his belt buckle and—damn him!—he began to do just that.

Charlie had never been self-conscious about his body before.

He'd never minded women studying him naked. While he personally didn't think men's bodies were nearly as impressive as women's, he'd always been proud of his lean, hard physique and the muscles that he could flex with ease.

He'd never even minded them tracing the nicks and gouges and scars from his rough-and-tumble past. They'd been badges of honor, signs of his toughness and determination to survive.

That was then.

Now it wasn't the same.

His body wasn't the same, he realized about the time he began to unbuckle his belt. It was no longer lithe and fit and supple. His wounded leg, with its angry red scar tissue and atrophied muscles was nothing to admire. On the contrary, the very sight of it would probably put Cait off. So would the scar on his chest.

A couple of years from now, they might look like badges of honor. Right now they looked like hell, and he realized that he didn't want to show them to anybody—much less the one woman in the world he wanted to impress.

Too bad you didn't think of that sooner, he mocked himself, because Cait, having taken his dare, was standing there, barefoot and unblinking, watching him.

His hands hesitated at the top of his zipper. He imagined opening it, then shoving his jeans down, and watching her look of shock and horror.

He imagined her comparing his body with that of her cardiologist boyfriend. Charlie couldn't believe the guy was a real hunk, but he probably wasn't a walking disaster, either.

Slowly his hands fell to his sides. He shook his head. "Never mind."

Cait did blink then. "Never mind?" She gaped. "Why?"

He shrugged irritably and jerked his head toward the sky behind her. "There's a storm brewing." The clouds creeping over the tops of the Bridgers were bigger and darker looking now. "You should get home."

Cait didn't even glance over her shoulder. "There was a storm brewing two minutes ago."

"Yeah, well, I forgot you would have to ride all that way. Open air. Tall object. Lightning strikes. It took a while, but I finally figured it out. I'm a city boy, remember? Go on now. Or you'll get soaked."

But Cait, damn her, didn't budge. She was regarding him closely. "Charlie, are you all right?"

"Of course I'm all right!" He glared at her. "Why wouldn't I be?"

"Your leg—"

"My leg's fine. I told you. I just had second thoughts. I know enough to get in out of the rain, even if you don't!"

When she still didn't move, he shrugged. "Well, fine, stand there. I don't care. Show's over. If you're not goin' home, that's your problem. I'm outa here."

He would have turned on his heel and stalked up the hill, but doing so would have sent him sprawling. Instead he carefully turned sideways and then sideways again, until he could head back the way he'd come.

As he climbed the slope he listened for the sound of her putting on her boots or her footsteps heading toward her horse. He didn't hear anything until he was close to the top of the hill.

Then she called out, "Show's over? Doesn't look to me like it even started!"

The trouble with being a nurse was you felt so *responsible.*

You saw someone hurting and you felt compelled to help.

If she were sane and sensible and *not* a nurse, Cait told herself, she would be home reading a book or playing cribbage with her father this evening instead of climbing the steps to the McCalls' cabin and banging on the door.

"It's open," Charlie's voice called from inside.

She turned the knob and gave the door a shove.

To say that he was surprised to see her would have been an understatement. He was lying on the bed, still wearing the dusty, torn jeans and shirt he'd been wearing this afternoon, and at the sight of her he sat up abruptly and said, "Well, hell."

"Nice to see you again, too," Cait said crisply. She stepped inside and shut the door behind her. One look at him told her she'd been right.

"You haven't even washed up," she accused him.

"Excuse me?"

Cait flipped a hand in his direction. "Look at you. You're a mess. Still. Don't they have running water up here? Of course they do. Then why didn't you use it? You shouldn't even be up here walking around on that leg. Sit on the edge of the bed and take your shirt and jeans off."

She didn't look in his direction when she spoke, instead rummaged in her duffel bag, then set out a plastic bottle of saline solution and some telfa pads and gauze, determined that her professional demeanor would distract from any telltale heat in her face.

"Take my—" Charlie began.

"Take your shirt and jeans off. I'll be right back." she said and hurried out the door.

She'd ridden home mortified at her afternoon encounter with Charlie at the swimming hole. But the longer she'd been home, the less she'd thought about her own mortification and the more she'd thought about Charlie instead.

He had clearly been ready to strip off in front of her, and then he'd abruptly changed his mind.

Why?

Obviously because it hurt too damn much, and he was self-conscious about it. Stupid man!

She'd told herself it served him right. But she was a nurse.

Concern had niggled at her all during dinner. Afterwards, she usually tried to get her father to play cribbage. Tonight he had looked surprised when she said she'd be back later, that she had to go back up on the range instead.

She had loaded up their cooler with ice, ice packs and flexible wraps, then tossed in her duffel with medical supplies and some nonprescription painkillers just in case.

"Somethin' wrong with one of the horses?" her father had asked

"One of the mules," Cait had muttered, which was close to the truth.

Now she got the cooler out of the back of her pickup, slammed the gate and lugged the cooler up the hill toward the cabin.

Charlie came to the door as she was climbing the steps. "For God's sake, Cait!" He hobbled to help her.

"I'm fine. Stay out of my way." She hauled the thing past him and set it on the floor. "There." She opened it, took out one of the ice packs and a thin cloth wrap, then straightened up and looked at him expectantly. "Jeans, Charlie," she reminded him.

''Cait,'' he said, voice strangled.

She lifted a brow. ''Or maybe *you're* the one who's afraid?''

Their gazes met. Lightning seemed to flash, and Cait wondered if she had made a big mistake.

Charlie ground his teeth and, muttering, fumbled to unfasten his belt.

Cait clenched the ice pack, strove to look indifferent—and steeled herself for the sight of Charlie Seeks Elk unwrapped.

Four

It shouldn't have been like this.

It should have been him seducing her, them getting naked together. Not him shucking his clothes while Cait bustled around like some damned efficient nurse, setting out gauze and bandages and tapping her foot and looking like she had a hot date in half an hour—with Cardiology Man.

Okay, so she *was* a nurse.

She wasn't indifferent.

She'd loved him, for crying out loud! She'd stroked and touched his body in ways that had made his heart gallop and his body sing.

And now she was acting like he was a floor she'd been hired to scrub.

Yeah, well, let's see how long her indifference lasted.

Charlie tried not to think about his ugly leg or the scars on his chest and back as he pulled his shirt out of his jeans. He took his time, watching her all the while he unbuttoned it, then pulled it off and tossed it on the bed.

She didn't even glance his way. She was filling a plastic bag with ice and wrapping it in a cloth. She didn't even seem to notice the red scar on the front of his shoulder.

"You can put this on your leg," she said as she finished with the ice pack, "while I clean up your cuts."

"Don't you want to hold it on my leg, Cait?" He tried to put a little purr in his voice. Sometimes he used to tease her just to watch her blush.

But this time she simply said, "I'm sure you can manage. Then she glanced at her watch, not at him. "I'm meeting Steve for the late movie, so if we could hurry things along..."

Steve again. Damn Steve.

"Tell me about him," Charlie said. Not because he gave a damn, but it always helped to understand your competition.

Cait looked surprised. Then she hesitated a moment before she said, "He's tall, dark and handsome. He got his medical degree from Columbia. He's a cardiologist, like I told you. He's been practicing in Bozeman for the past four years, doing a little satellite work in Livingston. But he wants to teach and he's been asked to join a bigger practice in Denver, so he's going this August." She lifted her chin. "And I'll be going there this fall. After the wedding."

Charlie's eyes narrowed. "When's the wedding?"

"October 17. Before the snow. After shipping. Are you going to take those jeans off or not?" Cait demanded. She was tossing the ice pack back and forth between her hands, looking like she couldn't care less.

And all thoughts of "the competition" went right out of Charlie's head. Annoyed, goaded—and at the same time worried that she'd take one look at his leg and run—he shoved the jeans down his hips, then kicked them off and stood glaring at her as she finally looked his way.

"Pretty, isn't it?" His voice was gruff and defiant. He watched her face for signs of revulsion.

"Oh, Charlie." The words came involuntarily, he knew. And while he didn't want her pity, he was oddly grateful to see that she seemed to care.

Rather than running, in fact, she took a step closer. "Where exactly does it hurt?" she asked, and she put her hands on him. Her very cold hands.

Charlie almost jumped out of his boxer shorts. "Cripes, woman!"

But she ignored his protests. "Hush," she said, stroking his thigh gently. "Sit on the table."

He swallowed, willed his body to behave itself. Then he did as she said.

Cait began gently probing his leg, making *him* suck in his breath this time. And now that the initial shock had passed, he was breathless only partly because of the cold. He'd forgotten how good she smelled. Her hair was almost under his nose. The curve of her breast brushed his arm as she bent to study his leg. And her hands—cold though they were—were making him crazy.

"Here?" she said touching the knotted muscle. "I can feel the tension here."

"Mmm," Charlie stifled a moan.

"Sorry. Anywhere else?" She had her hand on his thigh, kneading it gently, then lifted it and slid her hand beneath, probing lightly.

The moan had nothing to do with his pain, and at her continued probing and stroking, Charlie very nearly moaned again. "Ah…um…yeah, there." His fingers clenched against the table. He shut his eyes and threw his head back.

The scent of her filled his nostrils. Juniper and sage and something indefinably Cait that even in the desert of Abuk spoke of Montana and reminded him now of the nights he'd held her in his arms.

They'd slept together in one narrow bed, Cait curled against him, exhausted from her long days at the hospital. Though he'd often been bushed, too, Charlie hadn't always slept. Sometimes he hadn't wanted to sleep. Sometimes he'd just lain awake and held her, storing up the moments, savoring them, convinced—and determined—that they were all he'd ever have.

God, he'd been a fool.

Now he was damned sure not settling for that. His heart knew it. His mind knew it. And his body very definitely knew it.

Cait must know it, too. Not many of a guy's secrets remained hidden in a pair of boxer shorts!

"Right. We'll need two."

"Two?" His head jerked; his eyes opened. He gaped.

She rolled her eyes. "Ice packs." She lifted his leg, slid the one ice pack under it, then went back to fill another.

"Oh." Charlie felt cold and bereft. His boxer shorts wavered. His body was in conflict. It wanted Cait. It didn't want more ice.

And then she was back, and naturally he got the ice.

"Hold this," she commanded. Then she put two fingers under his chin and lifted and turned his head so she could study his lip. "You could have washed at least."

"I drank whiskey," Charlie told her. "It's sterile."

Cait made a humphing sound. "Sit still." And she set to work.

She washed all his cuts and scratches with saline solution. She was brisk and efficient and not exactly gentle.

"Hey!" Charlie protested when it felt as if she were using elbow grease on a particularly dirty spot.

"Don't be a baby." And she scrubbed harder. "And stop groaning."

"I can't."

"I'm not scrubbing that hard!"

"The groans have nothing to do with scrubbing," Charlie told her, and was gratified to see the color rise in her cheeks. But, "Cait!" he protested when her scrubbing grew even more intense.

"There." She nodded her satisfaction when she'd scrubbed him down almost to the bone.

He touched his elbow gingerly. "Hurts worse now than it did when you started."

"But it won't get infected." She was cleaning up now, putting everything back in her duffel, then going to wash her hands.

Watching her taut shoulders and stiff back, Charlie was sure she wasn't as indifferent as she pretended. "Thank you, Cait," he said softly.

She had her hands under the water tap and she didn't turn around, but he saw her shoulders stiffen even more. "You're welcome."

He wished he dared go to her, put his hands on her shoulders and knead them gently. He used to do that when she got off work. And she would tip her head back and run her lips along the line of his jaw and make mmmmm sounds that set his hormones singing.

It was all he could do to stay where he was on the table. But he managed it.

She cleaned up and said, "Keep those ice packs on there twenty minutes at a time. Do it every few hours. I put in enough ice that you should have some until midday tomorrow."

"All right."

"Did the doctor give you stretching exercises?"

"Yes."

"Are you doing them?"

"Trying to."

"Do them."

"All right."

She looked at him narrowly, almost suspiciously.

Charlie smiled at her.

She averted her gaze and rubbed her hands on the sides of her jeans. "Fine," she said briskly. "I'll leave you to it."

The smile vanished. "And go to the movies with your fiancé."

"Yes."

He looked at her narrowly. "Going to sit in the back and neck with him?"

"Charlie!"

Her shocked face made him grin. "Sorry. I should know better. You'd never do a thing like that."

They had once gone to a political documentary in an old battered theatre in Abuk only so they could kiss in the back row because two of Charlie's journalist buddies happened to be sacked out in his apartment.

The sight of Cait's flaming face told him she remembered, too. He cocked his head and grinned at her.

"Goodbye, Charlie," she said through her teeth.

"Bye." He waited until she was going out the door. "Cait?"

She turned to look at him.

"Think of me."

"I think I'd like triplets," Mary Holt said the next afternoon. Cait was listening to her belly with a stethoscope, but staring off into space. "Or maybe quintuplets. That'd be fun, don't you think?"

"Hmm? Mmm, yeah. Sure," Cait said.

"All boys," Mary went on cheerfully. "Little hellions. Just like Gus. That'd be terrific."

"Yeah."

"And you can be their godmother and baby-sitter. Okay?"

Cait nodded absently. "Okay."

"You haven't heard a word I said."

At Mary's indignant accusation, Cait had the grace to blush. "I'm sorry. I was...listening to the heart beat."

"Only one?"

"You want more?"

"No. But I just told you I thought quints would be nice—all like Gus—and you agreed with me."

"Yikes." Cait shrugged guiltily.

Mary laughed. "My feelings exactly."

"He's a good foreman, though," Cait allowed. She'd hired Gus Holt this past winter right before he and Mary had tied the knot. He'd been apprehensive at first, worried that maybe for all his having grown up on a ranch, he wouldn't be up to the job.

But Cait had had faith in him. She'd seen how conscientious he'd been with Mary when she'd been pregnant. He hadn't known anything about expectant mothers, either, but he'd set out to learn.

"If you try as hard for the ranch as you did with Mary, you'll do fine," she'd told him.

And he had. He and Mary had moved into the old homestead on the Cutter place, which her father had bought a few years back. No one had lived there since and the house was almost falling down. But Gus and Mary had taken it on eagerly.

"It will be a great place to raise a family," Mary had said, seeing possibilities that were beyond Cait. In the past few months they had turned it into a home. And now they were going to have the family to enjoy it.

Mary was two and a half months along, bubbling, eager, and "only sick until noon," she reported ruefully.

"You're doing great," Cait told her now. "You look wonderful."

"You don't."

Cait blinked. "What?"

"You look worried." Mary sat up and pulled down her shirt. "Is it your dad?"

Cait shook her head. She made some notes on Mary's chart. "Dad's all right."

"Is it Steve?"

Cait looked up quickly. "What about Steve?"

Mary smiled. "Aha."

Cait set the pen on the counter and stuffed her hands in her pockets. "What do you mean, aha? Steve is fine," she said defensively.

"Or at least he was the last time you saw him," Mary said, disgusted.

"He's busy! *I'm* busy!"

"Busiest two people on earth," Mary said dryly. She stood up and adjusted her clothing, then laid a hand on Cait's arm. "Take time for each other. You need to. You're working too hard."

"I have to work hard. I've got the ranch as well as my practice and—"

"—as long as you're busy, you don't have to deal with the wedding."

"What?"

"You heard me. Maybe it's my imagination, but it looks to me like you're stalling."

"Stalling? I'm not stalling!"

"Well, you're not exactly rushing to the altar."

"Because we're not horny teenagers with stars in our eyes like some people."

Mary grimaced. "Point taken."

"I didn't mean that," Cait said hastily, remembering that Mary and Gus had been teenagers in love once upon a time. At least Mary had been. She'd had stars in her eyes, too. Gus had had cold feet. It had taken him nearly a dozen years to warm them up.

"Steve and I are adults," Cait said calmly. "We're waiting until the time is right. October isn't so far away."

"October?" Mary brightened. "You've set a date, then?"

"Yes. Well, sort of. I think." She'd picked a date out of the air when Charlie had asked her yesterday.

She didn't want him to think she was "stalling" like Mary did, and she knew he'd jump to that very conclusion if she admitted they didn't have a date carved in stone.

Besides, the more she thought about it, October 17 seemed as good a day as any.

It was, as she'd told Charlie, after shipping and before the snow flew—more or less. It would give Steve time to get settled in Denver and comfortable in his job, and it would give her time to breathe for a minute or two after the herd had been shipped. It would also give her time to wind down her practice and make sure her dad was really capable of running the place.

"When? Where? Can I help?" Mary was all eagerness.

"October 17," she said firmly. "We're still deciding where."

Steve would be delighted. He'd been eager to set a date since he'd given her a ring. She was the one who'd hesitated, worrying about her father mostly. How could she say she'd go to Denver when he was still so ill?

He wasn't *that* ill, Steve had maintained. He was taking advantage of her.

Cait had never believed that, but maybe Steve was right. In any case he'd be delighted when she told him tonight.

They were going to dinner. They hadn't gone to the movies last night. She'd called him when she got home from Charlie's to see if he wanted to. He might have, after all. Saying they were going had been for Charlie's benefit. And they could have, except he'd been on call and had had an emergency.

"Well, I'm glad you've got a date finally," Mary said. "I'll help."

"I think you'll have quite enough to do getting ready for this baby and teaching school."

"I might have a little free time. I'm not directing the Christmas pageant this year," Mary said. "I've already told Polly that. She seemed relieved," she added with a grin.

Last year Mary had not only directed Elmer's community Christmas pageant, but brought the house down by nearly delivering a baby in the middle of it.

"I suppose she would be," Cait said with a smile. "Who's she going to get?"

It was always a challenge finding a suck—er, volunteer—to take on Elmer's holiday extravaganza. Polly McMaster, Elmer's postmistress and long-suffering mayor, had to strong-arm someone into doing it. Last year she'd conned Mary, the community's newest and therefore most unsuspecting resident, into the job.

"It's a rite of passage," she'd told Mary. "You'll always belong once you've suf—er, done—it."

Mary had agreed, and she'd done it very well. She'd also cemented her place forever in Elmer folklore by her near delivery on stage. She'd made it to the hospital, but she'd also managed to convince Polly that pregnant pageant directors were probably not a good thing.

"Don't know who she'll get this year," Mary said. "Just breathe a sigh of relief that it won't be you."

It took Cait a moment to realize what Mary meant—that it couldn't possibly be her because she'd be gone.

She felt oddly bereft at the thought. She'd missed lots of Elmer's pageants over the years, but she'd remembered the ones she'd seen as a kid with great fondness. She'd told Resi about it. And Charlie.

She shoved away the thought. "Maybe we'll get back for it, come see Dad for Christmas. It's not so far."

"That'd be wonderful," Mary said. "I hope so. Your dad would be so happy. We'll take good care of him for you." She put her hand on Cait's and gave it a squeeze.

"I know. Get Arlene to make you an appointment for a month from now," she said as Mary started toward the door.

Mary's face fell. "I just realized, you won't be here to deliver the baby."

Cait smiled ruefully. "I know. I wish I could . Maybe I—"

"No. You're not putting it off," Mary said flatly. "Between you and Steve, you'd let the entire state's medical welfare dictate your wedding day."

"Hippocratic oath," Cait grinned.

"Whatever. You're not changing it. And I expect you to let me know what you want me to do. Gus and I will be happy to help. Anything at all. Don't hesitate to ask. We owe you."

"Thanks."

But Cait imagined that even Gus might draw the line at chasing Charlie out of town with a shotgun.

Charlie hesitated before he mounted the steps to the broad porch that ran along the southeast side of the Blasingame ranch house.

He'd promised himself he wouldn't push Cait, and he was on her doorstep less than twenty-four hours later. But he was returning her ice cooler.

Returning the ice cooler wasn't pushing, was it? It was being responsible. Adult. And she might need it.

Besides, he wanted to tell her about the bears. He'd

found them again today. Picking some kind of berries. It reminded him of that children's book *Blueberries for Sal* that he'd read over and over to Chase and Joanna's kids. He got some pictures their seven-year-old, Annie, would love.

Cait would love them, too.

He could hardly wait to tell her.

He left before the bears did this time. He'd been more careful to watch where he walked. His leg hurt, but it was better. Some better.

Maybe a little sore.

Maybe he could get Cait to put some more ice on it today.

He set the cooler on the porch and rapped on the back door. At least, he thought it was the back door. It also looked to be where all the activity took place. There were two pairs of boots by the door. Beside an old milk can and a stack of newspapers weighted down by a rock sat a box of veterinary supplies. Alongside them were some cans of motor oil, as if someone had been doing various chores and didn't quite finish.

Cait?

He didn't ever remember her expertise extending to car mechanics. But who knew?

He peered through the curtained glass of the door as best he could, looking for signs of life. It was dinnertime. He figured that was the best time to catch her home. But she didn't seem to be answering, and he hadn't seen her truck when he pulled in.

Maybe she was teaching a class tonight. Or maybe a baby was being born.

Or maybe she had another hot date with Cardiology Man.

Charlie gritted his teeth. He knocked again. Harder.

There was no response. He paced a small circle on the

porch, jammed his hands into his pockets, glowered at the shut door, then kicked the post by the steps.

Chase would tell him he was being too impatient, that he was ''doing,'' not ''being.'' But for Charlie, ''being'' was damned hard work.

He sighed and started to go back down the steps. He'd reached the bottom when he heard the door rattle open behind him.

He turned back, a smile and the words he'd planned forming on his lips—and dying there—at the sight of an older man.

''Help you?'' In his jeans and faded plaid shirt he looked like a stereotype of a cowboy. His short, once dark hair was salty with gray now. His lined face was weatherbeaten, battered by the elements that doubtless made him appear older than he was. He looked like someone right out of those full-color cigarette ads. Except for the bedroom slippers he wore.

He looked tired. As if Charlie had woken him up. His eyes were flat and disinterested. They were blue, but they were the same shape as Cait's.

Charlie hadn't considered her old man. Of course he knew her father lived there, but he'd only been thinking about Cait.

Now he rethought quickly. What had Cait told him? Had she mentioned his name? And in what context? He couldn't imagine her having said anything positive. And he didn't want the old man having another heart attack on his account.

''Hi,'' he said, ''I, uh, am a friend of Cait's. I've been staying at McCalls' and I was returning her cooler.''

The old man looked at Charlie, then at the cooler, then said, ''You cowboyin' for Otis an' Jed?''

Otis, Charlie knew, was Brenna McCall's father. He

shook his head. "Not...exactly. I'm a photographer. I'm just staying in their cabin."

The old man frowned. "You an artist?"

"Sort of. I don't do the same stuff. I do...*did*—" he corrected himself "—harsher subjects. Wars and urban violence. Inhumanity," he said awkwardly.

The old man's face lit up. "You're Charlie Seeks Elk?"

Taken aback by his suddenly beaming face and the quickening interest in his eyes, Charlie could only nod.

Cait's father, clearly delighted, was coming down the step, holding out a hand. "Caity said she knew you," he said, real animation in his voice for the first time, "but I didn't know she meant you were friends!" He grabbed Charlie's hand and pumped it up and down. "Mighty glad to meet you. Come on in."

Since he didn't let go of Charlie's hand as he went back up the steps, Charlie didn't have much choice. And since the old man was anything but ready to blow him away, Charlie went along quite happily.

"I'm Walt Blasingame, Cait's dad," the old man said, ushering Charlie into the kitchen and crushing his hand one last time before waving him toward a seat at the round oak table by the window.

"Pleased to meet you, Mr. Blasingame."

"Walt," the old man corrected. "Call me Walt."

"Walt." Charlie put a chair between himself and Cait's dad. "You say Cait...mentioned me?"

"She's got your book. *Inhumanity.* That's how I knew. How 'bout a cup of coffee? You want to stay for supper? Of course you do. Cait'd never forgive me if I let you leave without invitin' you for a meal." He was talking as much to himself as Charlie as he started running the water and filling the coffeemaker.

"She has my book?"

"Sure does. Damn fine book." Walt Blasingame

thumped the coffeepot down for emphasis. "You make a feller think."

"Er, thank you." Charlie couldn't help blinking at Cait's father's unexpected enthusiasm. Had he got it from Cait? Somehow Charlie doubted that.

"Sit down. Sit down," Walt Blasingame urged.

Charlie sat. He looked around the kitchen, feeling oddly as if he'd been here before.

Then he remembered that Cait had often talked about family meals right here at this table. He rubbed his finger along the edge and felt the tiny ridges that she once told him she'd carved to figure out a tricky math problem.

"My dad said to figure it out myself," she'd told him. "And when I did and he found out how, he tanned my backside."

The recollection made Charlie smile. The whole room made him smile. It was a warm, friendly sort of room. Homey. Comfortable. Different in style, but similar in feeling to the kitchen at Chase and Joanna's house.

Walt grabbed a cookie jar off the counter and dumped a pile of homemade oatmeal cookies on a plate, then stuck them in front of Charlie. "Help yourself. Where'd you come from? How come you're at the cabin? Ain't no wars in Montana. Not at the moment anyhow." He chuckled, then fixed Charlie with an avid look. "So what brung you?"

I came to marry your daughter.

Probably not the best place to start.

Charlie stalled, taking a cookie and biting off a chunk. It was ambrosial. When he'd finished it, he said, "I came from California. I'm just here for a while. A little R&R. Hadn't ever been to Montana before, and I remembered Cait talking about it..."

Walt beamed. "The last best place, that's what they call it. You like it?"

"Yeah," Charlie said, surprised at how true it was. "Yeah, I do."

"Good cookies, aren't they?" Walt poured two mugs full of strong black coffee and carried them to the table. "Cait made 'em. How'd you meet Cait?"

"I was taking some photos near the hospital where she worked."

"The one in Abuk?" Walt shook his head and grimaced. "She don't say much about it, but I reckon it was pretty bad." He sat down opposite Charlie and wrapped callused fingers around his coffee mug.

"It had its moments," Charlie allowed.

"I was in Vietnam. I know there are things you don't just toss into conversation, but...I'd like to understand a little more. She gets real quiet sometimes. An' I wonder if I can help. Will you tell me?"

"Er." Charlie swallowed. Tell him what, exactly? "What did you want to know?"

Walt pushed back his chair. "I'll get the book."

He came back moments later with an obviously well-read copy of *Inhumanity.* "Cait said she bought it 'cause of the little girl," he said. "But she don't want to look at it," he said. "Leastways, not when I'm around."

I wonder why, Charlie thought, mocking himself.

"Says she knew the little girl." Walt patted the cover picture of Resi with her sad wide eyes.

"Yeah." And for the first time in months, Charlie made himself look at Resi's picture. If it was possible to feel even more guilty than he did about what had happened between him and Cait, it was what he felt about Resi. He had betrayed her love, her trust, possibly her very life—to protect his own emotions.

"Lucky little gal," Walt said now.

"Lucky?"

"Well, not lucky in the first place," Walt qualified.

"Losin' her folks. Gettin' hurt like that. But in the end..." He got a sort of sad, wistful smile on his face.

Charlie felt his heart skip. "In the end? What happened in the end?"

Walt looked surprised. "You didn't know? Why she got a new home! A new family. Somebody adopted her. One of Cait's friends."

Charlie stared. "One of— *Who?*"

Walt shrugged. "Dunno the name. Cait said it, but I don't recall. Said she was one of the lucky ones." Walt rubbed the side of his thumb over Resi's photo, and his mouth twisted slightly. "Some of 'em ain't. People turn their backs on 'em."

"Yeah." Charlie felt hollow, and yet reprieved at the same time. Like he'd been acquitted when he knew he was guilty as charged.

Resi had been adopted? And Cait knew the family?

He tried to think who it might be.

Another one of the American medical staff? Her roommate, that girl from Tulsa, Jessie? That eye surgeon who worked miracles on a daily basis? He had a hundred notions. All possible. But none had seemed likely when Cait had suggested they marry and adopt her themselves.

Was Cait pleased now? She'd loved Resi, had wanted her for her own.

Had wanted both him and Resi.

And it was his fault she didn't have her.

"Cait can tell you who, I reckon," Walt said. "Here, now. Let me dish up dinner. Cait made stew an' it's keepin' warm. Don't usually feel much like eatin', myself. But long as you're here..."

"Is Cait...teaching tonight? Or delivering a baby?"

"Don't think so," Walt said. He got out plates and put half a loaf of bread on the table. "To mop up with," he said. "She an' that doc were goin' out."

"That doc? Her…fiancé?"

"Yep. Steve. Nice feller. Busier'n a one-armed paper-hanger. My Lord, he didn't hardly stop to say hello when he was doin' his rounds in the hospital. But he's a good doc. An' I reckon it's like that when so many folks are dependin' on you."

"I guess," Charlie said slowly. He'd wanted Walt to say Steve was a jerk.

"'Bout time they got a night to themselves," Walt said instead. "Too busy, the two of 'em, takin' care of everybody else." He eyed Charlie over the plate of stew he'd just put in front of him. "Reckon she went up last night and took care of you."

Charlie felt a faint heat in his face. "I got shot a few months back. Tore me up pretty bad. I fell yesterday. Ran into Cait afterward, and next thing I knew she was bringing me ice."

Walt smiled. "That's Caity. Wes, my boy, always used to call her Caity the Bandage Lady. She was forever patchin' him up when they were kids. Caity patches everybody up."

Charlie didn't want to hear that, either. He wanted to think she had done it because it was him.

"Eat up now," Walt said. "Then maybe you could tell me some about those pictures."

They ate in companionable silence. Cait's stew was wonderful—far better than anything he would have cooked for himself. When they finished eating they did up the dishes together and then he followed Walt into the pine-paneled living room to talk about the pictures.

Once more he had the sense of having been here before. Cait had talked about this room, too—about sprawling on the braided rug on the floor and watching cartoons on television, about building cabins with Lincoln logs by the fireplace, about the bookcases against the wall that her grandfather had built.

"My books were on the bottom shelf," she said. "And on winter days I used to sit in the chair by the fire and read them."

He could just imagine her there—a smaller, more freckled version of Cait curled in the leather armchair, deep in a book, her long dark hair in a braid that she nibbled on the end of during the exciting parts of the book.

Walt sat down on the sofa and Charlie took a seat next to him. He never minded talking about his photos, making his point. But this was different.

Walt opened the book to a photo of the devastation wrought by a grenade. "I saw buildings tore up like that," he said. His expression grew distant, his gaze far away.

This wasn't about Abuk, Charlie realized. The inhumanity was universal. It was Walt's way of dealing with all that he had seen.

They looked. They talked. Not so much in words, but in silences.

"There were children in Vietnam, too," Walt said. "Hurt same as that little girl you knew. Babies. Some of them soldiers weren't more than kids themselves."

Charlie stared at pictures he'd taken of soldiers who weren't more than kids. He hadn't been a whole lot more than a kid himself.

"Didn't know no more than kids," Walt was saying quietly. He stared unseeing out into the twilight. "Fella's scared he does some stupid things."

Yes. Yes, he sure as hell did. Charlie stared at Resi's sad, reproachful eyes and made himself confront the child and the reality he'd left behind.

In fact she, like Cait, had been in his heart ever since. He hadn't left her behind at all.

Then, in Walt's silence, he began to speak. Slowly.

"The first time I saw her," he said, swallowing past the sudden ache in his throat, "she wouldn't talk. She would only stare. And Cait brought me to see her because she thought I could do something. She thought I could help, that even if I couldn't help Resi, I could tell the world."

It all came back as he spoke—all the emotions, all the pain. Not just Resi's; everyone's. Abuk had been full of pain in those days. People lost. People hurting. People dying.

And yet, in midst of that pain, for a few isolated moments, there had been joy. Not just the joy of knowing Cait.

There had been joy with Resi, too.

No, there had been no words. But there had been growth. Eye contact. Her first wavering smile. Her tentative touch. And finally, the morning he found that tiny stuffed bear and brought it to her, the first words that broke a silence of God knew how long.

He could still feel her small trusting fingers curving around his. He could remember the light in her eyes when he walked into the room.

The light had flickered out early on that morning when he'd come to tell her that he had to leave.

Had to leave!

He stopped talking and just sat staring into space. He thought of all the things he'd done wrong. All the ways he'd tried so desperately to protect himself, to assure himself he was doing the right thing for all of them.

What a liar he'd been.

He didn't notice the tear that streaked his cheek. Or feel the muscle tick in his temple. Or hear Walt's quiet words.

Or wonder what they meant when the old man said, "I know. I know."

Five

Steve was thrilled at the news. ''Well,'' he'd said. ''Finally.''

''It's all right?'' Cait twisted her napkin nervously in her hands as she looked at him over the table at Sage's. ''The date, I mean?''

Steve said, ''Sure, fine.'' He grinned. ''I'll shut off my beeper all day. Just kidding.'' He consulted his small day planner and did some mental figuring. ''Perfect, as a matter of fact. I'll tell them I'll be gone a week. That way we can go on a quick honeymoon and I'll be back in time to fly out to Johannesburg for the conference on the twenty-sixth. Couldn't have planned it better myself. What inspired you?''

Somehow telling him about Charlie didn't seem like a particularly good idea.

''It was time,'' Cait said. ''I mean, if we're going to do it, we ought to just do it. Right?'' She gave him a brilliant smile.

"Absolutely." Steve reached across the table and gave her hand a squeeze. "That's great. You can come with me down to Denver the weekend after next and we can find a place to live."

Cait blinked. "What?"

"You come with me," Steve said. "For the weekend. Since we're actually going to do it this fall, wherever I am is going to be your place, too. No sense in me renting something for a couple of months and then us moving. You'd better come along, too."

Cait hadn't thought that far ahead. She also wasn't at all sure she should leave her father for a weekend. "We'll see," she said.

"Come on. Start planning now," Steve cajoled her, "and we can probably pull it off."

"I'll have to talk to my dad. Maybe we could take him with us?"

Steve didn't look extraordinarily thrilled at the idea, but he nodded. And the notion of taking her father along actually pleased Cait a great deal.

He needed something to cheer him up. Too many nights recently she had come home to find him sitting in his chair staring into space or, worse, looking through Charlie's book, dinner still slow-cooking away.

"Not hungry," he'd say when she remonstrated with him. "I'm not all that interested in eatin', Caity."

He wasn't interested in much these days.

"It would be great to take my dad along," she said eagerly now, and glanced at her watch. "I really ought to get going. I wasn't home last night, either. And I won't be tomorrow because of my birthing class. I should be there to eat with him more often."

"He's got to learn to cope sometime, Cait," Steve said. "He won't do things for himself if he knows you'll do them for him."

"It isn't a matter of doing it for him," Cait said, because she'd already done that, though Steve didn't know it. "It's a matter of keeping him company. He's all alone."

"Then he needs to invite people over. Get out. See his friends."

"Yes." Cait agreed completely. But agreeing and convincing her father to do it were two different things.

Brenna and Jed had invited him over several times. Unless Cait was there to go with him, he'd declined. Gus and Mary had invited him, too, but he hadn't gone. And he wouldn't invite anyone in.

Just last night she'd suggested he call Otis Jamison to come over and play cribbage while she was hauling the ice up to Charlie.

But Walt had said he was too tired. "Maybe another night," he'd said vaguely.

Cait lived in hope, but not much.

So she was surprised to drive into the yard that night and see Otis Jamison's old Suburban parked near the barn.

"Well, finally," she said, relieved. Maybe her going out last night and tonight was actually doing some good by forcing her father to seek out his friends if he wanted any companionship at all.

She opened the back door and went into the kitchen. A look around made her smile widen. Obviously he'd eaten. And had company for dinner, too. She could see that the slow cooker had been washed out and there were two sets of silverware and plates drying in the rack by the sink.

There were voices in the living room. She pushed open the door and breezed in. "Hi! You're still up! I'm so glad Ot—"

She stopped dead at the sight of Charlie.

Her father thumped his book down on the coffee table and looked up beaming. "Ah, Caity, look who's here!"

Charlie, who knew better than to beam, smiled determinedly as he got to his feet. "Hey. Out catching babies tonight?"

"What are you doing here?" Cait demanded.

Her father's eyes widened at her tone. "Caity! Where are your manners?"

Cait bit back the reply that sprang to her lips. "I'm just…surprised to see him here." She kept her accusing glare for Charlie, who was looking like innocence personified.

"I brought back your ice chest."

"You needn't have bothered."

"Well, I wanted to say thanks. And," he grinned faintly, "I was sort of hoping for more ice."

"Staying off your leg would do more good than coming clear over here."

"Can't do that. Gotta keep an eye on those bears. Besides, I am taking care of it. I watched where I was going today."

"Still—"

"I didn't wear it out. I had a good day. Took some shots of bears and berries." He grinned. "And then I brought the cooler back."

It all sounded very straightforward. But Cait didn't believe for a minute that was all there was to it. There was a look in Charlie's eyes that she recognized all too well. It was the same look he got whenever he'd been hot on the trail of good photos.

But she couldn't challenge him now—not with her father such an avid spectator.

"Well, thank you," she said grudgingly.

"I invited him to stay for supper," her father said cheerfully, looking brighter than she'd seen him in months. "Was sorry you missed him. But I asked him to stick around. Figured you'd want to see 'im. An' after we ate, we set out here an' talked."

Which sounded rather ominous. What had Charlie been telling her father? What had her father told Charlie?

"Well," she said briskly, "thank you for bringing the ice chest back. If you need some more I'll give you some and—"

"I'll live without it," Charlie said. "I really came to see you. To thank you." He was looking at her intently, so intently she had to look away.

Nervously she began to straighten the magazines on the coffee table. "You're welcome," she said. "But you didn't need to come all this way for that."

"It was the least I could do."

"No, it wasn't. You could have ignored me completely."

"Caity wouldn't do that. She'd never turn her back on a friend," her father said cheerfully. "Don't know why you didn't tell me where you were goin' last night," he said to her.

Cait lined up the magazines in precise rows. "It wasn't important."

"Not compared to your hot date," Charlie said.

Cait saw her father's eyes go wide. "Hot date?"

"Steve and I were going to see a movie," Cait told him, shooting Charlie an annoyed glance. "But Steve had an emergency, so I just came back here instead. We went out tonight," she said for Charlie's benefit.

His brows lifted and he glanced at the clock. "You're home early." The implication being that the date hadn't been all that hot.

"I thought Dad was alone," Cait said irritably. "Obviously, I was wrong. So thank you for staying and keeping him company. You don't have to hang around now."

Her father was positively sputtering at her rudeness.

Charlie seemed completely unfazed. "Oh, I enjoyed it. We had a good time. Besides, I sort of felt like I already knew you a little,'' he said to Walt. ''Cait told me a lot of stories.''

''Did she?'' Her father was smiling like the Cheshire Cat. Then he fixed his gaze on Cait. ''You,'' he accused, ''didn't tell me anything.''

''You were hardly in any shape to be entertained by my war stories when I got here. You were in Intensive Care.''

''Well, after,'' Walt grumbled. ''You sure never said anything much about this feller here.''

Cait didn't look at Charlie. She shrugged. ''I had nothing to say.'' Then she did glance at him and added dismissively, ''Charlie was in and out of my life so quickly.''

''And now I'm back,'' Charlie said.

''Briefly,'' Cait acknowledged. She yawned widely, doing nothing to mask it, hoping he would take the hint. When he didn't move, she said to her father, ''I'm tired. I think I'll turn in.''

Her father gave her a disapproving look, which Cait determinedly ignored. Instead she dropped a light kiss on his cheek, then turned to Charlie. ''Thank you for returning the cooler.''

''Have dinner with me tomorrow night.''

She stared for a split second. ''What?''

''Have dinner with me.'' He repeated the words she hadn't wanted to hear in the first place.

''No. Thank you.''

Her father looked shocked. ''Caity!''

''I've got things to do.''

''He's an old friend.''

''I'm teaching tomorrow night. My birthing class.''

''After your class,'' Charlie said, all accommodation.

''I don't finish until nine.''

''I'm allowed up after nine,'' Charlie said with gentle mockery, making her father chuckle and Cait furious.

''I'm engaged,'' she hissed at him.

"So? He won't let you have dinner with an old friend?"

"He doesn't have anything to say about it!"

"Well, then..." Charlie spread his hands. "Old friends need to catch up."

Friends? Cait looked at him skeptically.

"You're engaged. What else could we be?"

She glared at him. "Dad will be alone again and—"

"Enjoying every minute of it," her father cut in firmly. "You don't need to rush home on account of me, Caity girl. I'm feelin' fine."

Surprisingly he looked brighter, as if he'd taken a turn for the better, as if something had come along to inspire him.

Charlie?

Surely not!

"You might not be feeling good tomorrow night."

"Humph," her father snorted. "I reckon I'll survive. Quitcher fussin' and g'wan out with Charlie."

Quit her fussing? Cait gaped at him. Who had been demanding that she hover over him like a broody hen for months and months? Who had been saying he just wanted her around? Who had felt too poorly to be left alone?

Now he looked brighter than she'd seen him in ages. There was a hint of life and challenge in his eyes—as if he were daring her to have dinner with Charlie.

"Fine," she said shortly. "Be at the hospital at nine."

"If I come early can I check out your class?"

She blinked. "You want to watch a bunch of expectant mothers breathe and pant?"

"I like to see women pant." Charlie grinned, and her father smothered a chuckle.

"Come ahead then," Cait dared him. "I'll put you to work."

Charlie grinned. "I'll count on it."

* * *

Cait tossed and turned all night. It was because of the wedding, of course. She'd never planned a wedding before. She had so many things to think about. The wedding itself, the reception, the music, the flowers, her bridesmaids, the guest list.

Charlie.

She shoved the thought of him away. But, as persistent in her mind as he was in person, he came right back. "Fine," she muttered, crushing her pillow against her chest and staring at the ceiling. "I'll invite you. You can watch me marry Steve. You can eat your heart out."

Oh, yes. Sure he would.

She knew better. He was pushing her now because he thought he wanted her. If she ever said yes, she'd marry him, he'd turn and run so fast she'd be left staring at his dust.

Well, she wasn't going to say yes to Charlie. She'd already said yes to Steve. She just wished Charlie would go away and leave her alone.

She hadn't been thrilled to see him with her father tonight. She wasn't thrilled to know he was meeting her for dinner tonight. If she could have called him up and declined later, she would have. But the McCalls' cabin had no phone, and if he had a cellular, she didn't know his number.

So she spent the day hoping he wouldn't show up.

But at seven that evening he was standing outside the classroom, waiting, when Cait came around the corner.

The very sight of him caused that familiar quiver deep inside that she always felt when she saw Charlie. She used to think it meant she was in love with him. Now she knew better. It was just a hormonal response to a handsome man. It had nothing to do with love.

"You're early," she said.

"I'm interested."

"In a bunch of pregnant women?"

"And their teacher."

She felt her cheeks warm. "Don't, Charlie." She brushed past him to go into the classroom.

"I'm telling the truth, that's all."

"We're friends, remember? That's what you said. If you're changing the rules, you can leave right now."

He shrugged. "Fine, we're friends." He followed her to the front of the room and caught her hand before she could jerk it away. "We were always friends, Cait."

They had been. It was she who had wanted more, who had hoped for more, had thought they had more. She tugged to get her hand away from him, but he didn't let go, and she knew he wouldn't until she agreed with him.

"All right," she said, annoyed, "we're friends."

"Good. I thought maybe I could take some pictures."

"Of what?"

"Your students."

She stared at him to see if he was joking, but he seemed perfectly serious. "I've been doing a lot of moms these days. And kids." He glanced around. "Maybe a few dads, too. Relationships."

"Relationships?" Cait said doubtfully. That didn't sound like Charlie.

He nodded. "What you need to pass on. Connections. That sort of thing. What mama bear taught her young 'uns. I saw this elk with her calf this morning." A delighted grin lit his face. "Coolest thing." Then he looked a little embarrassed, as if his enthusiasm betrayed him. But finally he just shrugged. "I'm working it out as I go along. Photographing what interests me."

"Moms and kids?" Cait said, allowing herself to sound sarcastic.

"Yeah. I'm just gathering material. I'll look for the themes later."

"I thought you had a theme—inhumanity."

"Had," Charlie agreed, propping one hip against the edge of the counter that ran along beneath the windows. "But there's more to the world, thank God. More I need—*want*—to explore." He looked reflective for a moment, then continued. "I've seen enough inhumanity, God knows. I've helped other people see it. That's what my work was, what my book was. But after I got shot, well, I started thinking there was a lot of life I hadn't ever focused on. I'd only half lived. Gaby told me it was time to move on. She's right."

Cait was surprised at his sincerity. Still, it was hard to imagine Charlie doing mothers and babies. They were the opposite of everything he'd done before. Positive, not negative. Life affirming, not a record of death and destruction. Harbingers of hope, not despair. And they were usually settled.

Charlie had never been settled. She had seen that, in retrospect. He'd always been restless, eager to be moving, dashing here and there, intent on what was just over the next hill or in tomorrow's news.

"I'll ask my students if they mind," she said. "I'll introduce you to them and we'll see. We've got seven moms in all." She nodded toward the back of the room where they were beginning to congregate.

Most, of course, brought their husbands or boyfriends, but occasionally they brought a friend or a relative. After all, Mary had brought Gus before they were married or even really going together again. The birthing class had brought them together.

"And damn near frustrated the life out of me," Gus had told her ruefully not long ago. "But at the time it was the only way I could get my hands on her."

Cait had never thought of her class as an erotic experience before and had said so.

"It's all in the mind of the beholder," Gus had told her with a wink and a grin.

Cait was determined not to let any erotic thoughts cross her mind. She'd had plenty about Charlie in the past, but that was over. All her thoughts were for Steve now.

Charlie was just part of the furniture. He could hang around. She would even go to dinner with him. But that was as far as it would go.

Finally the last couple arrived—Angie Mayhew, barely seventeen and the youngest of the moms-to-be, came in with her coach and foster mother Maddie Fletcher, seventy-five if she was a day. Angie was looking her normally sulky self, but long-suffering Maddie was beaming as always.

"Sorry we're late," she apologized.

Angie kept on scowling until she saw Charlie, then her normally truculent expression changed and her gaze grew interested, speculative.

Cait felt an even greater than normal irritation with the girl. Putting it aside, she cleared her throat. "We have a visitor today, a friend of mine from California, Charlie Seeks Elk. Charlie is a professional photographer, and he's asked if you would allow him to take some photos of our session. I'm not exactly sure what he has in mind, so I'll let him explain what he wants to do."

If Charlie was surprised that she put him on the spot, he didn't give any indication. He looked up from tightening the lens on his camera and grinned that beguiling Charlie grin that, within minutes, had everyone eating out of his hand.

He used to take pictures of grim stuff, he told them. Misery and pain, he said, had been the hallmarks of his work. And then he'd seen the light. "I finally figured out that if I only focused on that, I was missing a big part of life," he told them, "the best part. I shot a lot of photos of death and dying. Now I'd like to look at the other side. So I'd like to take some photos here—of birth and getting ready for it. Unplanned. Unposed. If I get good ones, with your permission, I'll hang them in a show I'm doing down in Santa Fe next spring. What do you say?''

The women, except Angie, looked embarrassed, but nodded. Angie preened. Charlie, Cait could tell, noticed.

''Just ignore me,'' he said to all of them. ''Listen to Cait and pretend I'm not here.''

It was like telling them not to think of pink chickens, Cait thought. *Whatever you do, don't think of pink chickens!*

Charlie was the most noticeable pink chicken in the room. They eyed him warily out of the corners of their eyes. They glanced back over their shoulders to see where he was and what he was doing.

In fact, Charlie wasn't doing anything. He was holding his camera, but he wasn't shooting. He just held it easily in his hands and waited for Cait to start.

Cait was as self-conscious as her students. Maybe more so. But everything depended on her, so she began. This was the third week of the six-week course. The time of birth was getting close now. Several of the women were experiencing contractions. One had already been hospitalized overnight when labor had appeared imminent.

It was time to give them a view of what to expect instead of just talking about it. ''We're going to look at a video first tonight,'' she told them. ''A time lapse of labor and delivery so you know what to expect. You can see the breathing techniques in practice and watch for the transitions. It will help make some sort of sense of what we've been doing.''

As she talked, she, too, flicked glance after glance in Charlie's direction, but he still wasn't moving, just listening. Everyone else—except Angie—had stopped turning around by this time.

She expected Charlie to wander off during the video or possibly shoot some low-light photos, but he never lifted his camera once. Instead, once the film started, he stayed right where he was, perched on the counter at the side of the room, and watched, entranced, as the on-screen labor progressed.

Everyone else watched the movie, too. Cait watched him.

She'd seen the movie already—about a dozen times. That was her excuse. There was also a little curiosity about Charlie's reaction. She'd seen him tender and gentle with Resi, but she knew better than anyone that he never really got involved. So it was a little surprising that he looked almost shaken when the video ended with the mother holding her brand-new child in her arms.

The other viewer who sat in complete silence was Angie. She looked scared to death.

About time, Cait thought.

The girl's cavalier attitude and general flippancy had irritated her from the start. Only the fact that Maddie had come with her, determinedly supportive and making up for Angie's general rudeness had convinced Cait to put up with her in the class.

"All right," she said after punching Rewind on the VCR. "Now that you've seen what you're in for, let's get to work again on some of the breathing techniques. Everyone get a mat."

Charlie began to move around the room, taking pictures as everyone got a mat. The pregnant women, grumbling and laughing at their own awkwardness, lowered themselves to the floor. Their coaches knelt beside them, all except Maddie who was moving a little slowly.

"It's these damned arthritic knees," she said with an

expression halfway between a grimace and a grin. "I'm not as young as I used to be."

Angie was looking impatient, not helping at all.

"Here," Charlie said to Maddie, dragging over a chair beside the mat where Angie sat. "You sit here."

"I'm supposed to help," Maddie protested.

"You can help from there," Charlie said firmly. "If you need anything done on the floor, I'll do it."

"She's supposed to put her hands on my belly," Angie informed him with a sly, speculative look.

Charlie just shrugged. "I can do that."

Angie brightened considerably, and Cait felt an unpleasant and unwanted shaft of annoyance spear her. She turned her back and began to start the breathing sequence. "Okay, everyone. Let's go."

She didn't think Charlie took another picture for the rest of the class, but he did manage to keep Angie focused on what she was supposed to be doing. Of course she was doing it to impress Charlie, but at least she was doing it. She had only come to the earlier classes because Maddie had insisted.

"I'm leading the horse to water," Maddie had told Cait privately. "God knows if she'll drink."

She would, Cait decided irritably, if Charlie was around to help her.

She tried not to notice them as she went around the room, helping out each couple who had questions. Naturally Angie didn't have any questions. Except for Charlie.

Even after the class was over and the mats put away, Angie was sticking close to Charlie, her expression equal parts lust and hero worship as she followed his every move with her eyes. Charlie was talking to Maddie, but he was smiling at Angie and resting a hand on her shoulder.

Cait grabbed the video out of the VCR and stuffed it in

her tote bag. Then she strode across the room. ''I'm ready,'' she said bluntly.

Charlie turned his smile on her. ''So am I.''

She steeled herself against it, then turned to Maddie and Angie. ''See you next week.''

''Yes,'' Maddie said, then took Charlie's hand. ''Thanks from my old knees.''

Angie grabbed his other hand. ''You're coming back next week, aren't you?'' This from the girl who hadn't wanted to be there in the first place.

Charlie slanted a glance in Cait's direction. ''If she'll let me.''

Cait's jaw tightened, and she had to force herself to smile. ''As long as you don't upset things.''

''He won't!'' Angie assured her eagerly. ''He's a big help.''

Cait raised her brows in a look of polite skepticism.

But Maddie smiled as she gave Cait's hand a squeeze. ''He's a big help,'' she agreed.

Cait wasn't so sure about that. She knew all about being led on by Charlie Seeks Elk, who, even when he had no intention of doing so, had a disastrous effect on the opposite sex.

''Come on, Angie,'' Maddie said now. ''We've got to get going.''

''You're coming, right?'' Angie insisted, looking imploringly at Charlie.

He gave a quick nod. ''If it helps, I'll be here.''

Satisfied for the moment at least, Angie left with Maddie, actually smiling for the first time since Cait had met her.

''Well, you've certainly made an impression on her,'' she said gruffly, leading the way out of the classroom and down the corridor.

Charlie fell into step beside her. "Nice to make an impression on someone."

"Just don't be leading her on."

"I don't lead women on."

"You might not try to. Sometimes it just happens. And Angie is susceptible."

"I've got the point," Charlie said. He paused. "Where's her man?"

Cait snorted. "He's not much of a man. He took off when he found out she was pregnant. Then her family kicked her out. She lived with a girlfriend for a while, then she started flirting with the girlfriend's boyfriend and got kicked out of there. She ended up in Bozeman and someone got hold of Martha Reese. Martha is a social worker. She got Maddie to take her in. Maddie's been bringing her here, trying to convince her to help herself and to take care of herself. She hasn't been exactly willing."

"I know the feeling," Charlie said with such quiet intensity that Cait looked sideways at him. His jaw was tight and there was a grim look in his eyes. She remembered what he'd told her about his own past and realized that he would feel a certain empathy for Angie.

"Then you realize how vulnerable she is."

Charlie nodded.

Cait hoped so. She didn't want to see Angie hurt further. The girl already had a big enough chip on her shoulder, and whatever Maddie and she and Martha had tried to do for her had fallen on deaf ears.

"Where do you want to go to eat?" Charlie asked when they reached the parking lot.

Cait had given that considerable thought. It had to be the right setting. She knew Charlie wouldn't settle for any of the fast-food places tonight, and she didn't want to go to a more expensive, intimate restaurant. That would make this look—and feel—too much like the date it wasn't.

"The Barrel," she told him. "It's a place to go with a friend."

"It's a bar," he protested.

"How do you know?" she said, surprised.

"I've been there." He didn't explain further, just scowled, then shrugged. "If that's what you want, let's go." He started toward the silver Porsche he had obviously traded for Otis's Suburban tonight.

But Cait wasn't riding in any Porsche with Charlie. "I'll meet you there."

He scowled again, but finally he nodded. "Suit yourself."

"Yes." Cait was determined she would.

The Barrel was noisy and cheerful. There were pool games going on in the back and a crowded bar up front. Many of the tables were filled, and Cait seemed to know a lot of people there. She stopped to talk to half a dozen, casually introducing him as a friend from L.A. whom she'd met overseas. It seemed to him she came down harder than necessary on the word *friend.*

Everybody nodded and said hello. One or two of the women looked at him with that sort of look that good-looking men come to recognize after a while. It said they were interested. And one or two of them were pretty enough to interest most men.

Not him.

"Come join us," one of them, a sweet-smiling brunette, invited.

Cait smiled. "Thanks. We'd love—"

"—to, but we've got some catching up to do." Charlie gave the woman a nod and a smile, took hold of Cait's arm and steered her right on past.

"How rude was that?" Cait muttered.

"I don't know. How rude was it?" Charlie found them

a relatively secluded table, pulled out the chair facing away from the room so she couldn't spend time looking for a little help from her friends, and waited until she had no alternative but to sit in the chair he held for her.

Like the gentleman he could be when he chose, he pushed it in for her and took the seat opposite. "There now. Isn't this nice?"

Cait looked as if she didn't know what to say to that.

Charlie was pleased. "I liked your class."

"Makes you want to run right out and have a baby, hmm?"

"Made me aware of how strong women are. I'd never seen a baby born before."

Chase had told him that, after his firstborn twins, Emerson and Alexander, arrived, if he'd known what *labor* really meant he would never have got Joanna pregnant.

Charlie, a clueless nineteen-year-old at the time, hadn't given it much thought. Sex was fun, that was all he knew. That it could be better when people loved each other, he'd supposed might be true. At least Chase and Joanna's relationship seemed to imply that it was. But the consequences for the woman had never really hit home until he watched that video tonight.

He couldn't quite imagine watching Cait go through that.

"It's hard work," he said, which was putting it mildly.

Cait nodded. "But it's only the start. Raising them is harder."

"Yeah." He smiled faintly. "Just ask mother bear."

"Did you see her again?"

He nodded. "This afternoon. Your dad showed me a good spying spot."

She looked startled. "My dad?"

"Yeah. He came by this morning just as I was leaving

to look for the bears again.'' He could tell that surprised her. ''Why? Don't you want us fraternizing?''

But she looked bewildered, not angry. ''I'm just...I can't imagine what he was doing up there.'' She shook her head. ''He's barely left the house since he got home from the hospital after his heart attack.''

''I thought that was last summer.''

''Last fall. He was in the hospital until early October. He came home right before round-up. He wasn't well enough to do that, and after round-up it was cold, and I didn't encourage him. I thought he'd start doing things again come spring. But he didn't. He's just been sitting at home staring out the window or...'' She paused and didn't finish the sentence. ''He actually came up to the cabin? Did he say what he was doing up there?''

''Came to check on some cattle, he said.''

Cait stared. ''He didn't drive his truck? He *rode?*'' Now she looked alarmed.

Charlie shrugged. ''He seemed to do all right. We rode up to some creek above your pasture and then we walked and—''

Her jaw sagged. ''He *walked?*''

''He's not at death's door, Cait!'' Charlie protested, but now he was starting to get worried, too.

''I need to call him,'' Cait said. ''To see if he's all right. Whatever did you say to him yesterday that would have made him do that?''

''What did *I* say to him?''

But she had jumped up and was heading for the phone, leaving Charlie to hurry after her.

Walt answered the phone. From the conversation, at first solicitous and concerned on Cait's end and finally terse, Charlie gathered that Walt had assured Cait that he was fine. ''I am not fussing!'' she protested. ''Fine. Goodbye.''

She got off the phone a few minutes later looking miffed

and perplexed both. "He acts like it was a perfectly normal thing for him to do," she muttered, heading back to their table.

Charlie shrugged. "Maybe it was."

But Cait was shaking her head. "To just get up after all these months and go see you to show you where he'd seen some bears?" Cait's eyes narrowed. "What did you talk about?"

"Bears."

"That's all?"

He thought about it. "My book," he added after a moment. "And Vietnam."

"He talked to you about Vietnam?"

"Yeah."

The waitress came over then and took their orders. When she left, Cait looked right at him and said, "He's never talked to anyone about Vietnam."

Charlie lifted his shoulders. "Sometimes it takes a while. You know as well as I do that what you see in places like that isn't something you come home and blab about."

Cait nodded. "Yes, but..." She paused. "But your book showed what it was like." She murmured the words, hesitated, then asked, "What did he say?"

"Just talked about how different everything was. The noises. The colors. How vivid it was. Like technicolor. Not the real world. Another world. Another universe."

Charlie had understood completely. Sometimes the places he'd been and the things he'd seen had seemed that way to him, too.

The waitress brought their beers and he wrapped a hand around his glass. "He talked about the people. Guys in his outfit. People who lived there. A teacher he'd met. He asked if I ever got close to the people where I worked."

Their eyes met, and there was no doubt they were both remembering how close they'd been.

Then abruptly Cait looked away. She picked up her glass and turned her head to stare across the room, to watch the pool players and the barmaids. The jukebox moaned a loved-'em-and-left-'em song.

Charlie ran his tongue over his lips. "We talked about Resi."

It seemed, for just an instant, as if there was the hard click of pool ball on pool ball—and then silence.

He laid his hands flat on the table and looked across it at her. "We haven't talked about Resi."

She swallowed. Her knuckles were white on her glass. She lifted her shoulders in a tiny shrug, as if doing any more than that would hurt too much. It hurt him to see it. He knew he deserved to be hurt.

"Why should we talk about Resi," she said evenly after a moment.

"Because she matters."

"To me."

"And to me, too. Though," he admitted, "I was afraid to let her matter too much."

She looked surprised, but she didn't say anything.

"Your dad says some friends of yours adopted her?"

Cait nodded. "Morse and his wife."

Charlie stared. "*Morse?* Morse Griffin? Mr. I'm-on-the-Next-Plane-Out-of-Here Griffin? Mr. Nothing-Touches-Me Griffin?"

"Resi touched him," Cait said simply.

He just sat there, stunned. Of all the people they'd known in Abuk who might have done such a thing, Morse Griffin was the last person Charlie would have expected to do it. Although he was married, Morse seemed to have had even itchier feet that Charlie had.

"Are they…is it…" He couldn't seem to find the words. "Are *you* all right with that?"

"Of course I'm all right with it," Cait said sharply. "Morse and Jeannie are good parents."

"Yeah, but…" His voice trailed off and he shook his head. "You wanted…"

"I wanted to adopt her. But I was single, and that wasn't going to fly. The government had certain requirements."

"Yeah. But Morse? I never would have figured." Charlie gave another disbelieving half laugh. "He didn't have a near-death experience, did he?"

"Not exactly." The waitress arrived then, bringing them steaks and salad. Cait waited until she had departed before continuing. "Part of Morse's being on the go all the time wasn't because he loved it so much. It was to avoid being home."

Charlie cocked a brow. "And now that they have Resi, that's all changed?" It didn't seem likely.

But Cait nodded. Her eyes softened. "Actually, yes." She smiled faintly. "Because he was finally able to give Jeannie what she wanted—a child."

Charlie stared. The song was a hard-driving Brooks and Dunn number now. Someone was whooping at the bar. He sat very still, thinking it through. "You mean…Jeannie wanted kids and…Morse couldn't have 'em?"

Cait folded her hands on the table. "Yes."

The implications of that took a moment to sink in. "Whoa."

"It happens," Cait said almost defensively. "It doesn't make him less of a man."

Intellectually Charlie agreed with her. But he *was* a man—and he could guess how the knowledge that he was shooting blanks would make Morse feel.

He sat back in his chair, took a breath and let it out

slowly. "A guy would have to come to terms with it," he said at last. "And it might take a while."

"It did. And I don't know that he would ever have considered adoption if it hadn't been Resi. But she was there…needing a home…and well, when you stopped coming in to see her, he started. It just sort of went from there."

Morse was the one he'd roped into grabbing his news van and taking him to the airport the morning he'd left. All the way there Morse had badgered him about where he was going, asking where on earth there was more devastation than they were seeing right there.

He'd thought Charlie was running *to* something, not away.

Finally at the airport he'd looked at Charlie narrowly and said, "There isn't anything urgent out there, is there?"

And Charlie had shrugged. "Just…gotta get away."

Morse had understood. Morse had stepped in. He'd done what Charlie couldn't do.

And he was now Resi's father.

"He never said," he muttered.

"It's not the sort of thing people talk about except to their nearest and dearest," Cait pointed out. "And sometimes not even then."

"Yeah." Charlie's steak was getting cold, and the waitress came and asked if everything was all right. He nodded and started to eat. It was good, he supposed. But he didn't taste it really. "Do you see them?" he asked finally.

Cait smiled. It was a little wistful, but not really unhappy. "I saw them in February. They adopted a baby boy. Travis Mark. They're very happy."

"Even Resi?"

"Resi most of all. She's done very well. She's almost seven now, you know. Starting second grade in the fall. A big girl, she told Morse and Jeannie, and tired of being an only child. She wanted a baby sister or brother.'' Cait's smile grew lopsided. ''She was ready to share. Travis is Resi's baby.''

Charlie could see tears in her eyes. He could feel them pricking behind the lids of his own. His throat squeezed shut on the steak he was trying to swallow. At least it saved him having to say something and the embarrassment of hearing his voice crack with emotion.

''So,'' Cait said finally, briskly, ''you did them a favor.''

''Yeah,'' Charlie said slowly.

It wasn't all that comforting a thought.

Six

She had handled it well. All of it.

She'd got through the birthing classes without letting Charlie see how aware of him she was. She'd survived last night's dinner at the Barrel very nicely. She'd even managed to talk about Resi with equanimity, stressing the positive aspects of her adoption. It was true, in fact, what she'd said when she told him he'd done them all a favor.

He'd done her a favor, too.

And she was determined to believe it.

"Earth to Ms. Blasingame." A teasing male voice infiltrated her consciousness above the hospital hub-bub that she routinely tuned out.

"Oh!" She glanced up from the paperwork she'd been staring at for the past ten minutes to see Steve grinning down at her. She shoved an escaping tendril of hair off her cheek and met his grin with a smile of her own. "Hi."

"Hi, yourself. Glad I caught you." He reached inside

his shirt pocket, pulled out a much-folded piece of paper and held it out to her. "Here."

Cait took it. "What's this?"

"Guest list. The start, anyway."

Cait, unfolding it, found her eyes widening. There were at least a hundred names. "The start?" she said when she had swallowed.

"Doctors at the hospitals here and in Bozeman. Their wives. Our office staff. A couple of the guys I play golf with… I figured, since we were getting sort of a late start, I should come up with something pretty quick. I talked to my mother last night. She has another hundred or so."

"Another…hundred?"

"That's not a problem, is it?"

"I, er, no. I just…hadn't given it a lot of thought." Frankly, thinking about it was terrifying. What did she know about planning a wedding?

"I'll help," Steve said. "And my mother said she'd fly out from Boston any time you want her to. She's thrilled. She was sure I was playing some sort of practical joke on her when I said we were getting married but could never come up with a date."

Cait had only met Steve's mother once. Carolyn Carmichael was The World's Most Organized Woman and she liked nothing better than to prove it by organizing people. Cait didn't need a human bulldozer right now, no matter how eager and well-intentioned she was.

"Um, thanks." Cait managed a bright smile. "Tell her I'll be in touch. I…need to check some things out first."

"Right." Steve dropped a kiss on her hair, started to leave, then turned back. "Don't worry about the rehearsal dinner."

"Rehearsal dinner?" Cait hadn't even considered one.

Steve grinned. "That's my responsibility, my mother says. We'll take care of that."

She probably already had, Cait thought glumly. "Well, good. Something I can take off my list," she said with all the cheer she could muster.

"I'll call you when I get a full list," Steve said. "And we can—"

Mercifully whatever they were going to be able to do was cut off when his beeper sounded.

"Gotta run. Talk to you later." He bent once more and gave her a swift kiss before hurrying off toward the operating room.

Cait sat in silence staring at the list in her hand. Where on earth was she going to find a place to put two hundred of Steve's nearest and dearest friends and relatives? What was she going to feed them? Where would they all stay? A thousand panicky questions reeled through her mind.

Cait was calm under fire. She had patched up disaster victims, delivered a baby under bomb threats, stitched up dozens of seriously wounded men. She was good at a lot of things.

Planning weddings obviously wasn't one of them.

Besides, an extravaganza of a wedding wasn't what she'd ever had in mind. She'd always envisioned a small intimate gathering—her closest friends, her father, her brother Wes, a few cousins, Chase and Joanna and the few people who mattered to Charlie—

Charlie?

Cait broke out in a cold sweat. No! Not Charlie.

Steve! Steve, whom she loved! Steve whom she was going to marry!

Charlie, indeed!

How could her mind have played such a trick on her?

Furious, she stuffed the paperwork into her bag and stood up, her hands clammy and shaking. She needed some fresh air, less stress, the opportunity to talk to someone who could set her on the right track, someone who understood about weddings, who could steer her straight.

As soon as her appointments for the day were over, she got in her truck and drove to Mary Holt's.

What was a foreman's wife for if you couldn't go dump wedding jitters on her? Besides, Mary had said she'd help, hadn't she?

But Mary, looking aghast at the list Cait handed her, said, "Two hundred people? That's out of my league. We'll call Poppy. And Milly. They'll know what to do. Poppy's a pro."

Poppy Nichols ran a florist shop in Livingston called Poppy's Garden. She was, thus, something of an expert on weddings, and Cait could see calling her.

But Milly?

"Wasn't it Milly's wedding that Cash crashed and slugged the usher?" Visions of Charlie pulling a stunt like that almost brought out a cold sweat.

"That was her *first* wedding," Mary said. "The one Cash stopped. The one where she married him went all right, I think."

"Still," Cait hedged, "maybe we should just call Poppy."

Mary laughed. "Worried you might jinx things? That someone might crash *your* wedding?"

"God forbid."

"We could screen them all for weapons before they came in the church." Mary laughed.

"I'm sure Steve's mother would be impressed by that."

"The point of the wedding, my dear, is not your mother-in-law. If you've got the right man, you don't need anything else."

Cait felt a sudden tightening in her chest. "What do you mean?"

Mary blinked at the vehemence of her question. "Don't

take it personally,'' she said with a laugh. ''I was only saying that the groom is the most important thing.''

''Well, of course,'' Cait said, laughing it off. But the tight feeling eased only slightly.

''Don't worry about his mother.'' Mary reached out and patted her arm. ''You'll do fine. If you're worried, stop by the Mini-mart on your way home.''

''The Mini-mart?'' Cait stopped there for bread and milk and eggs when she forgot to go to the grocery store. ''Why?''

''You can buy all the latest bridal magazines there. Read two or three of those and you'll be an expert. You'll know the best places to go on a honeymoon, the right number of courses to serve at a very formal affair, the proper wording for invitations. They'll tell you exactly what to do and when.''

''Truly?'' Cait's education had obviously been lacking. She'd never read a bridal magazine in her life.

Mary grinned and crossed her heart. ''You will find everything in them you need to know. And then some. I promise.''

Cait wondered if it would tell her how to forget the wrong man.

''Whitelaw.'' The voice was fuzzed. Either the connection or—

''Hey, it's me,'' Charlie said.

Chase groaned. ''You all right?'' His voice became suddenly rough and intense the minute he recognized Charlie's on the other end of the transatlantic call.

''I'm all right.''

''All in one piece? Not shot?''

''No.''

''Then do you know what the hell time it is?''

''Er. Sorry.'' It was early evening in Montana, which

would make it, what? Somewhere around four in the morning at the villa on Lake Como where they were staying for the week. "But..."

But not all that sorry. He'd been stewing ever since this afternoon.

Walt had come by again. He'd been moving some cattle and he'd stopped "to set a spell," he told Charlie. And then he'd begun muttering about Cait telling him he'd have to wear a morning suit at the wedding.

"Hell," he'd said. "Didn't even wear a morning suit at my own weddin'."

He'd talked about hundreds of people and Cait figuring only the town hall would be big enough to hold them all and how he was going to have to be Walter Francis Blasingame on the invitations and how there wasn't a soul in the county who'd know who that was.

"Always been Walt," he'd said. "Always." He'd snorted. "Not even my sainted ma called me Walter Francis."

It had all sounded very definite to Charlie—and his policy of letting Cait come to her senses in her own time was looking pretty disastrous. When Walt left he'd paced around the cabin wondering if he was doing the right thing by not just going in and grabbing Cait by the hair and hauling her off.

"I mean, they did it to the Sabine women, didn't they?" he asked Chase now.

"Um," Chase mumbled. "Not so sure that's a good idea, pal."

"Well, I've got to do something!"

"Hang on." Charlie heard him say something quietly and heard Joanna's muffled sleepy reply.

"Tell him I love him," he heard.

"She loves you," Chase said a moment later. "But then," he added grimly, "she's not talking to you at four-fifteen in the morning, standing on a balcony in her undershorts.''

Charlie smiled. ''You're a good friend.''

''I'm more than a friend.''

''I know.'' He was the closest thing to a father Charlie had. He would have been Charlie's adopted father if Charlie had permitted it. He hadn't.

But Chase and Joanna hadn't let him turn away. They'd simply said, ''Fine. You don't want to be a Whitelaw, that's okay. But you're still part of the family.''

And despite his determination to hold himself aloof, he was.

''You're a good dad,'' Charlie said now.

There was a moment's silence. A long moment's silence.

Then, ''Well, thanks,'' Chase said at last. ''Now, let's see if I deserve the praise. What's up?''

''She's marryin' the wrong guy!''

''Not you, in other words,'' Chase said dryly.

''Not me. She's got bride magazines all over the house, according to her dad. She's talking about hundreds of people. Morning suits. Sit-down dinners.''

''Tell me about it,'' Chase muttered, and Charlie remembered the event that had been shoved down his and Joanna's throats.

''Then you know how serious it is,'' Charlie said. ''Nobody puts out that kind of effort and then backs out.''

''Joanna did,'' Chase reminded him.

''What? Oh, God, yeah.''

Charlie suddenly remembered that five years before Joanna and Chase were actually married, they had been engaged. They had gone through a huge society wedding right up to the vows and then Joanna had stopped.

She'd said, ''I can't.'' She'd run off and left Chase to do the explaining.

Now Charlie cursed himself for bringing it up quite like that. "Sorry," he muttered.

"Don't be. It was educational," Chase said. "I learned from it. You can, too. The point is—you can't force someone to marry you. I wanted to marry Joanna. But when push came to shove, she didn't want to marry me."

"She was too young." Charlie remembered that.

"For whatever reason, she didn't want to do it. She felt pressured and she went along with it—up to a point. And then she balked. You don't want your lady doing that to you."

"No."

God, no. He didn't want that.

"So take my advice, don't push. Don't grab her by the hair, throw her over your shoulder and attempt to make her see things your way. You weren't ready two years ago," Chase reminded him.

"I am now."

"And she's not. That happened to me and Joanna, too. When she was finally ready, I wasn't. I had just discovered that everything I thought I knew about my family wasn't really true. I needed to find out who I was before I could commit. It isn't going to work if it isn't right for both of you."

"You're saying, just wait?" Charlie was appalled. "Don't do *anything?*"

"Just wait," Chase said, exactly the way Charlie wished he wouldn't. "If it's going to happen, it's going to happen. You have to trust."

"What if," Charlie finally voiced his biggest fear, "she's never ready?"

"God help you," said Chase.

It would have been harder if it hadn't been for Walt.

He dropped by every day, inviting Charlie to accompany

him while he rode out to check some cattle or mend some fence. Sometimes he wanted to show Charlie a good spot from which to look for wildlife. Sometimes he thought maybe Charlie would like to know how to rope a calf or use a running iron.

Sometimes he just wanted to talk.

Most days Walt talked. About the ranch. About his wife, Margie, who had died ten years before, about his kids, Wes and Cait, about his hopes, about his dreams, about the war.

In the end, Charlie realized, it always came back to the war. The places he saw, the experiences he had, the people he met, the impact it had on life as he had known it back home.

"Sorta got engaged before I went to 'Nam," he told Charlie one afternoon. "Me an' Margie were this close to gettin' hitched." He held his fingers half an inch apart. "But I told her we'd better wait. Didn't want her sittin' there waitin' for me if I went missin' or grievin' if I got blowed to bits."

From everything Walt had said about his wife, Charlie suspected that Margie would have grieved whether or not they'd been married had Walt been "blowed to bits." But he didn't say so. He just rode Babe alongside the older man as they checked the fence line. And he listened.

"There now," Walt said nodding toward a loose wire in the fence, then dismounting to fix it. "No, sir," he said, eyeballing the slack wire, "didn't want her sittin' around waitin' if anything happened. Told her so. An' she said, 'I'll wait, Walt. You know I'll wait.' Hand me the splicer," he said to Charlie.

By now Charlie knew what to do. He handed over the splicer. He'd been watching Walt mend fences for the past five days. It was like watching a skillful surgeon. With years of practice, Walt made it look like child's play.

The first time Charlie had tried it, he'd scratched himself

on the wire and dropped the pliers, and the wire had sagged when he was done.

''Walt had watched in silence, then let him try it again, showing him how until Charlie finally got it right.

But today Walt needed to do something with his hands, apparently. So Charlie watched and handed, and Walt did it himself, by rote, not even thinking about it.

''Met a lot of people there,'' he went on. ''Women. Met this one lady schoolteacher. Pretty little thing. Sue, I called her. She wanted me to teach her English, said she wanted to come to the States sometime. Asked me all about it. I told her stories.''

Like Cait had told him stories? Charlie wondered. Had this young Vietnamese woman been as enchanted with Walt's stories as he had been with Cait's?

''Talkin' about it made it some easier,'' Walt said, splicing new wire in with the old. ''I liked talkin' to Sue. Made me a little less homesick. She was sweet and gentle—like Margie—and she laughed a lot. There we were in the middle of a war and sometimes she could still make me laugh.'' He shook his head, tested the wire, nodded his satisfaction and got back on his horse.

Charlie followed suit. They rode on.

''Sue was a sweet gal. And she was there. All I had from Margie was letters. Kept me from bein' homesick a little. But hell, sometimes it seemed like she was a million miles away. Reckon she must have thought that way about me, too. I figured she'd find someone else.'' He said the words more to himself than to Charlie.

They rode on. The breeze ruffled their shirtsleeves. The sun beat down on their backs.

''And then I got notice that I was gettin' some R&R,'' Walt told him. ''A week in Hawaii, they said. Sounded like a week in heaven. I wrote Margie and told her she could meet me there.'' He slanted a wry smile in Charlie's direction. ''You know, I really didn't reckon she would. I'd been gone a long time. She was just nineteen and damn pretty. Fellas were always sniffin' around. I figured she prob'ly had one and just hadn't told me 'cause of maybe makin' me walk in front of a bullet. I thought when I told her about Hawaii, I'd get a Dear John for sure.''

The horses picked their way along the line of the fence as it rose over a hill and down the other side.

Walt shook his head. ''But not from Margie. She wrote back, 'Name the day. Name the place. I'll be there.' An' five weeks later she was. R&R.'' He shook his head. ''Hell of a thing.''

Charlie understood what he meant. He'd been in a war zone one day and on a beach in Hawaii twenty-four hours later. It was mind-boggling. Unbelievable. It made you wonder what reality really was.

''We had six days. Sun an' sand an' each other. It didn't seem real. And yet it was more real than anything that had happened in 'Nam. She was real. We got married in Hawaii. First the honeymoon, then the weddin'.'' He smiled at the memory, and then the smile faded. ''An' then I got back on a plane to Vietnam and she went home to Montana, and I didn't see her for another year.''

''Must have been tough.''

Walt smiled faintly. ''You don't know the half of it.''

The last thing Cait wanted to do was ask Charlie for a favor.

But Maddie Fletcher had called this morning, and now she didn't have any choice. Of course, he might not show up.

She'd told Maddie that. ''I don't know if he'll even come to class. He might have got what he wanted.'' Photos, she meant, though she really didn't believe it much. It was just a subterfuge, just talk.

She knew Charlie hadn't got what he said he really wanted—her.

"Well, if he does," Maddie had persisted, "put it to him. Since he worked with Angie last week I've finally seen a spark of interest in her."

"Interest in Charlie," Cait translated and was still annoyed at the thought. It was purely on Angie's behalf, she told herself. She didn't want the girl getting all starry-eyed over a man who wasn't interested in her. Cait knew the feeling—had herself felt the humiliation of the consequences.

"Oh, absolutely," Maddie said with a smile in her voice. "But you learn, when you've been around kids like Angie as much as I have, to take any interest at all and go with it."

"You don't think it's…dangerous. I mean he's not interested in her."

"I know that," Maddie said. "I can see which way the wind blows."

Cait wondered which way Maddie thought the wind was blowing. But she refused to ask.

Maddie went on, "But if his being there, working with her, can get Angie involved, it will be good for the baby and good for her in the long run."

"But she'll expect—"

"You have to take things a step at a time, Cait," Maddie said. "We're not omniscient here. We can't play God. We can't see the end result. But we can do what we think best. In this case I think it's having Charlie work with Angie. And then we trust."

Trust Charlie?

Cait closed her eyes.

"So, would you ask him?" Maddie said after a moment. "I'd rather it was planned ahead of time."

Cait sighed. "If he shows up."

She still hoped he wouldn't. She hoped he'd got the point by now: that once upon a time she'd been interested in him enough to want to marry him—but he'd turned away, and now, when he said he was interested, she had, so to speak, other fish to fry.

No hard feelings. That was just the way it was.

She loved Steve. And all Charlie's persistence wasn't fazing her in the least. She didn't have time to even think about him. She was, with the help of a half a dozen bridal magazines, planning what her father had taken to calling "The Wedding That Ate Montana."

She had drawn up lists, called caterers, talked to Poppy about flowers, and had discussed with Polly McMaster renting the Elmer town hall. She had become a connoisseur of wedding invitations, formal and informal. She dreamed about ivory paper versus ash, rough edges versus smooth, italic versus bold. She chose type fonts in her sleep.

It was unutterably boring.

But it was better than dreaming about Charlie.

Why wasn't she dreaming about Steve? He was the man she loved, the man she was going to spend the rest of her life with, the man who had called just this afternoon to ask her to go to Denver with him this weekend to look for a place to live.

"It'd be great if you'd come," he said. "A whole weekend to ourselves."

It did sound great. But she didn't think she ought to leave her father that long, and she said so.

"He's going to be on his own when we get married," Steve reminded her.

"I know. I know. But he's just getting back on his feet. It's taken a while."

In fact, her father was progressing by leaps and bounds. He was riding again, checking cattle, mending fences, taking an interest in the ranch.

"He's doing stuff finally?" Steve said, obviously heartened. "When did this start?"

"A couple of weeks ago."

Ever since he'd met Charlie.

He was seeing way too much of Charlie. At first she'd attributed their encounters to Charlie turning up where her dad was. But from what her father said, that wasn't true. He was the one seeking out Charlie.

"Showed Charlie where I saw the bears last year," he said one day.

"Me 'n' Charlie rode up Hill Lake way," he said another. "I been showin' him how to mend fence."

Mend fence?

"You're teaching Charlie to mend fence?"

"He's turnin' into a fair hand," her father said. "Knows somethin' about horses. Learnin' about cattle. Quick study, he is."

What was going on? Why was Charlie turning himself into a cowboy? Why was her father taking such an interest in some tenderfoot urban photographer?

But she didn't ask, because she didn't want to know. She didn't want to talk about Charlie.

She hoped against hope that he wouldn't show up tonight. But she wasn't surprised to see him standing in the hallway waiting for her when she came around the corner.

He was leaning casually against the wall, his lean hard body looking relaxed and dangerous at the same time. He wore jeans and a long-sleeved blue chambray shirt—and boots, she noted now, irritated at how much he looked as if he belonged here. He straightened when he saw her coming, and she saw him wince just slightly as he shifted his weight onto his bad leg.

She didn't ask how it was. It was fine, she assured herself. He was riding with her father all day now. Besides, she didn't care.

He shoved a hand through the black hair which flopped onto his forehead. ''Hey.'' He grinned. It was the standard Charlie Seeks Elk heart-melting grin. She was sure women all over the world had fallen at his feet because of that grin.

It was a good thing she was completely resistant.

''Hey, yourself.'' She pasted on her best pleasant smile and said, as she had rehearsed, ''Maddie has a favor to ask. She wants you to continue to coach Angie.''

Charlie cocked his head. ''What does Angie want?''

''You in bed, I imagine,'' Cait said tartly. It was the bald-faced truth. She unlocked the door to the classroom, pushed it open and went in.

Charlie followed. ''Well, don't worry,'' he said, an amused tone in his voice. ''I'm a one-woman man.''

Cait bristled at him. ''Don't start, Charlie.''

He spread his hands, still grinning. ''I'm only saying.''

''Well, I'm *not* worrying! Not about you and—'' she floundered ''—and anyone!'' She took a deep breath. ''If you agree to coach her,'' she said evenly, ''I would just not want her reading more into it than you intend.''

''She won't.''

''How do you know?''

He shrugged. ''Because I won't let her.''

Like you didn't let me? Cait wanted to shout at him. But she twisted her fingers together and kept her thoughts to herself. ''Fine,'' she said tersely. ''Thank you.''

Charlie nodded, still smiling. ''You're welcome.''

Charlie understood Angie.

He had *been* Angie. Tough. Angry. Defensive. Determined to put up barriers to shut people out before they could do the same to him.

So he wasn't surprised when she looked less than thrilled when he said he was going to be her coach. She just hunched her shoulders and feigned indifference. "Whatever," she said and turned away.

Charlie didn't take it personally.

It gave him a new focus for practicing patience. He just smiled and dug in.

He worked with Angie, he joked with her, teased her gently, charmed her. He got her to let him take pictures of her. And at the same time he got her to pay attention to what Cait was teaching them. He got her to really work on her breathing.

And when he showed interest in the book on baby care that Cait gave all the expectant moms, she actually picked it up and began to look through it.

But she wouldn't smile, even when he tried to cajole her into it.

"What is there to smile about?" she demanded.

"You're alive. You're healthy. You have people who care about you." His gaze flicked to Maddie who was sitting a few yards away.

Angie saw where he was looking and hunched her shoulders. "She has to," she said gruffly. "They pay her to."

"Sweetheart," Charlie said, "nobody could pay anybody enough money to compensate for the guff they take from kids like me and you."

Angie's eyes went wide with surprise, then shuttered immediately. "What do you mean, me and you?" she asked suspiciously.

"You work hard tonight, and I'll tell you all about how you and I are alike," Charlie promised.

"When?"

"I'll come out to Maddie's place. You can cook me dinner tomorrow night."

"I don't cook," Angie informed him.

Charlie smiled. "You will."

He waited for Cait after class. Everyone else left—even Angie, after making sure he had directions to Maddie's place for tomorrow night.

"If you want to come," she'd said offhand, as if she really didn't care. But he could see it in her—the tiniest flicker of hope followed at once by the wariness that any reliance she put on someone would come to naught.

"I'll be there," he promised her. It was nice to have someone actually looking forward to seeing him.

Cait certainly wasn't.

He reminded himself to be patient. To give her reason to trust him. He'd given her plenty of reason not to.

But it wasn't easy. If he was patient too long, it would be October 18 and Cait would be Mrs. Dr. Steve Whoever.

Charlie gritted his teeth.

"I thought you'd left." Cait came out of the room carrying her tote bag. When she saw him waiting, she pulled it up against her chest and wrapped her arms across it, holding it like a shield as she locked the door.

"I wanted to give you my cell phone number."

She put the keys back in her bag. "What for?"

"So you can call me when Angie goes into labor. I told her I'd be there."

"I'm sure Maddie expects to handle that." She started down the hall. "She only wanted you for the classes."

He fell into step alongside her. "Well, she's getting me for both. She knows it. We talked." He held out a slip of paper with the number on it. "I gave it to her, too. But she might lose it in the excitement of the moment."

Cait stepped sideways, as if the paper might bite. But when Charlie persisted, she took it ungraciously and stuck it in her bag. She kept right on walking.

"Missed you this week," Charlie said. "But your dad says you've been busy."

"Lots to do for the wedding."

Sheer provocation. He could hear it in her voice. Like waving a red flag in front of a bull.

Charlie almost charged. He could very nearly feel Chase grabbing him by the scruff of the neck and hauling him back.

He took a breath and said instead, "Your dad's been teaching me to cowboy."

"I heard. I'm sure that will be very useful."

"Sarcasm doesn't become you, Cait."

She made a huffing sound.

"And you're right, it might." If worse came to worst, he figured, he might be able to build a loop, lasso her, then haul her away from her prospective groom. He had the sense not to say that, though.

They kept walking all the way to the lobby. The redheaded receptionist looked up with interest as Cait said in a very businesslike tone, "Thank you for your help this evening."

Charlie grinned. "My pleasure. Always a pleasure to see you."

Her shoulders stiffened. "Charlie," she warned. "This is about Angie."

"No, it's not. It's about us."

"There is no *us!*"

The redhead looked very interested.

"You gonna keep on lying to yourself right up till your wedding day?"

He could almost hear her teeth grind. He certainly could see the sparks in her eyes. And if looks could kill he knew he'd be on the critical list.

"Why are you doing this?" she said, anguished.

"Because I love you. Because you love me."

The redhead was almost leaning across the desk.

"No. I don't!"

The redhead didn't even have to strain her ears to hear that. Her eyes widened. She looked amazed.

"Damn it!" Cait hissed. "Now look what you've done!"

"What *I've* done? You're the one shouting."

"Because you...because...!" Cait sputtered furiously.

"Because you still love me and you're afraid to admit it!" Then, determined to prove it, he pulled her against him, tote bag and all, and kissed her for all he was worth.

Seven

So much for following advice.
So much for patience.
So he'd blown it.
Big-time.
What the hell was he supposed to do?
A guy couldn't just stand there and let a woman make the biggest mistake of her life without trying to stop her, could he?
And she would do it, too, he was sure! Charlie thought as he paced around the small cabin, which seemed almost to rock with the force of his emotions. Damn it, she would! She would have marched right down the aisle and married the hot-shot cardiologist, if Charlie hadn't stepped in and made his point.
So he'd made it, God help him.
He'd thrown caution—and patience—to the wind.
He'd kissed her.

He'd *needed* to kiss her.

He'd been living off memories and dreams and one single kiss since he'd found her again a few weeks ago.

He'd felt her hands on his body, he'd smelled the scent of her skin and her hair, but he'd never touched her the way a lover touches the woman of his dreams. He'd watched her lips, had dreamed about them, had remembered all too well the soft temptation of them. And he'd needed them the way he needed air.

He flung himself on his back on the hard, narrow bunk and stared up at the ceiling. He still remembered them. He still tasted them, hours later.

And he'd be living on that kiss for God knew how long!

She had softened under his onslaught. She had yielded, had opened, had given for a second or maybe a few. Not long enough, that was certain.

And then she'd stiffened. Her whole body had gone rigid, and she'd given him a shove. "Damn you, Charlie!" she'd said, her eyes flashing fire.

And then she'd spun on her heel and run out of the lobby, leaving Charlie and the receptionist staring after her.

In the silence that followed, the receptionist looked back at him, her expression unreadable. "Did it help?" she asked.

Charlie doubted that.

Probably he'd just shown her what a jerk he was. Nothing she didn't already know.

"I've changed my mind," Cait said the second Steve picked up the phone. She was gripping it as though it was a life preserver in a stormy sea, which in fact she felt it was. "I'd love to come with you to Denver."

"Huh, wha—Cait?"

He sounded dazed and disoriented, and she realized that, oh, hell, she'd done it again.

A quick glance at the clock told her it was two in the morning. She had been pacing around her bedroom for hours—after the long shower she'd taken when she got home had done nothing to erase the memory of Charlie's mouth on hers. Not even when she'd turned the tap to pure blue cold had she been able to forget, to make her body deny its response.

She'd tried telling herself after the first time Charlie had kissed her that she'd responded because he'd surprised her. The shock of seeing him had simply caught her unaware.

But she'd seen him coming tonight.

She'd felt the electricity sizzling between them all evening, although she'd done her best to stay well away. She'd deliberately ignored Angie for most of the evening because Charlie was helping her. She didn't want to encourage him, she told herself.

She hadn't dared admit she was afraid.

Not of him.

Of herself. Of her response. Of the fact that despite her common sense and determined indifference, she had been unable to put her attraction to Charlie away. And his kiss had completely undermined her resolve. It had made her ache with desire, with longing, with need.

It made her furious with him—and with herself!

And if cold showers and willpower were not going to do it, she would have to call up reinforcements. And that meant calling Steve.

She hadn't even thought to look at the clock. Damn. When was she going to stop waking Steve out of a sound sleep?

"I'm sorry," she apologized. "I didn't realize it was so late. So early, I mean."

She heard him yawn. "Never mind. 'S okay. What happened? How come you changed your mind?"

"I just...thought about it some more." She rubbed her fist across her still-tingling lips. "And I decided you were right. That's where we're going to be. And Dad's going to have to be on his own sometime. He might as well start now."

"Amen," Steve said, then added, "Truly, it is for the best, Cait. He needs to get interested in things again. Interested in doing them."

"He's been getting better," she said. "Every day he's doing a little more." All of it, she thought, gritting her teeth, with Charlie.

"Then letting him be on his own now is an excellent idea," Steve said. "You'll probably come home and discover he's got a new lease on life."

"That would be good."

"It will be good for all of us." He yawned again. "I'm glad you're coming, Cait. I didn't want to find a place without you. It's going to be our place, after all."

"Right."

Yes, definitely. Our place. Denver. Mrs. Steve Carmichael. She said the words over in her head, trying to imprint them there. "Go back to sleep," she said at last. "I'm sorry I bothered you. I just wanted you to know I'm coming with you to Denver."

"Love you," Steve said. "Talk to you tomorrow."

"Love you, too," Cait parroted. She hung up after he did.

She was still pressing her fist to her lips.

The cell phone's ring jarred him out of a fitful sleep.

At first Charlie couldn't even identify the sound. He'd been dreaming of making love to Cait—slow, languorous love—and then something rang. Like a timer. Like a buzzer.

Like—

He jerked up, heart pounding, cursing the alarm clock that was depriving him of the only contact he had with her.

Only it stopped.

And then it rang again.

He groaned and, realizing at last what it was, fumbled in the darkness to find his jacket and the pocket in which he'd stuck the phone.

Dire thoughts ran through his mind. Panicky thoughts.

It had to be Chase—or Joanna.

Any news in the blackness of night would not be good.

He jammed the on button in the dark and barked into the phone. "What? What is it?"

"Charlie?" The voice was strained, female. But not Joanna, thank God.

He felt a moment's shock, then confusion, as he realized who it was. "Cait?"

"Angie's gone into labor."

Charlie was stupefied. "Labor? She's in labor? *Now?* But she's not due yet. She's not due for...for weeks!"

"Welcome to the real world," Cait said. Her tone was crisp and almost businesslike, but the hint of tension was still there. "Babies are on their own timetable, not ours."

"But—"

"You don't have to come. We can manage without you."

She could, no doubt. And she would prefer it that way. He was less sure about Angie.

Still, he felt a surge of panic at the thought of coaching the girl through her labor. What the hell did he know about labor? He'd only been to two lessons! He wasn't the father! He'd been there because of Cait, because of the photos, not because of Angie!

Not *at first* because of Angie.

But now…

He reached for his jeans. "I'll meet you at the hospital."

If he'd had second thoughts—and he had plenty all the way over the mountain track in Otis's old Suburban, all the way along the curving gravel road to the county highway, all the way into the hospital parking lot in Livingston, even down the corridor to the birthing room—they vanished the moment he walked in the door.

Angie was lying in the bed, halfway elevated. Her normally pale complexion now rivaled the white of the sheets. Her dark eyes were wide and scared.

"Charlie! It's not supposed to be happening now!" She practically jumped out of the bed into his arms. But she was hooked up to a monitor, and he got to her before she inadvertently detached herself as she hurled herself at him.

Gone was the tough facade, the indifference, the determined nonchalance. Her thin arms went hard around his middle and she pressed her face into the denim jacket he wore. He wrapped his arms around her, hugging her tightly, then removing one hand to stroke her spiky hair.

"Hey," he said gently, "it's okay. It's what we trained for."

He felt her head shake against his chest. "Not ready," she muttered. "Not yet."

"Yeah," he said, giving her one fierce squeeze before letting her go so he could step back from the bed and look down into her frightened eyes. "Well, kids never do what parents want them to, do they? Welcome to motherhood."

She blanched even whiter at his words. He put his finger under her chin and tipped it up. "You can do it, Ang. Just be the kind of mother you always wished you had."

He saw her swallow and nod. Something of the toughness returned. But not the hardness. She bit her lower lip.

"Hurting?" he asked. He'd seen a lot of pain, but he had never, except in the film Cait had shown them, seen a child born.

"Not…really," Angie said. "My back sort of aches. I wouldn't even think I was gonna have it but I woke up in a puddle. I thought I'd wet the bed. Maddie heard me get up, and she came in and said my water broke."

Charlie only vaguely knew the logistics of labor and delivery. But he had the notion that unlike contractions, which might stop, Angie's water breaking meant there was no turning back. "Well, then, I guess this fella wants to be born."

Angie licked her lips. "I guess."

There was the sound of footsteps behind him, and Maddie and Cait came into the room. Maddie looked delighted at the sight of him.

Cait flicked a glance his way, then focused her attention on Angie. "Let's see how you're doing," she said. Her voice was calm and gentle, just the way he remembered it in the hospital in Abuk. It was one of the things he'd always admired about her—the way she could shut out the chaos that had often reigned around them and give her complete support and attention to the patient in need.

Angie looked nervously at Charlie.

He gave her hand a squeeze. "I'll wait outside with Maddie. We'll be right here. We're going to see you through this, all of us."

"I'm so glad you came," Maddie said, taking his hand as they went into the corridor. "It was such a shock. She'd been doing regular chores all day, nothing she hadn't done any other day. And you saw her just tonight—yesterday," she corrected herself because it was now close to four in the morning. "She was fine." There was an urgency in her voice that made him realize she was looking for reassurance.

He knew from what Walt had told him that Maddie and her husband, Ward, had taken in scads of foster kids over the years. They had devoted their lives and their ranch to helping kids who had hit a rough patch in their lives. Charlie knew she wouldn't want to think that something she had done had somehow caused Angie's premature labor.

"She was fine," he agreed. "You'll have to ask Cait, but it seems like it's just one of those things."

"Cait says that teenagers have more premature births."

"Do they have more trouble delivering?"

"I think they can." Maddie swiped a strand of gray-blond hair out of her eyes. "But Angie's healthy. She's strong." Now it was her turn to reassure him.

"She'll be fine," he agreed, as if it were a mantra, even as he prayed it would be true. "And so will the baby."

When Cait came out, her gaze went directly to Maddie. Charlie might as well not have been there. "She's doing well. Not having a lot of contractions yet, though she's dilating and the cervix is effaced. Still, it will be a while."

Maddie had questions for Cait. Charlie left them to it. He remembered his own time in the hospital all too well—and he knew what it was like to sit there, as the patient, while people talked about you outside the room. It had irritated him. He was pretty sure it would scare Angie.

She was still pale, but she looked a little less panicky now. "Cait says everything is coming along fine," she told him. There was a thready nervousness in her voice which implied that she wasn't sure Cait was right, but she was hoping.

"That's what she told us," Charlie said firmly. He came to stand right beside her, and when her hand moved restlessly on the sheet, he took it in his. Her fingers curved around his and clung.

They stayed like that for a long while. Neither spoke. Angie hung on. Charlie stayed where he was. His leg hurt. Every now and then he shifted his weight. But he never left, never gave her any indication that he was in pain.

When Maddie finally came in, she said briskly, "Get a chair, Charlie, and get one for me while you're at it."

When he did, she pulled the chair he brought over by the window away from the bed and took out her knitting. "This is supposed to be a baby blanket," she said, lifting the pastel bundle and settling it on her lap. "I'd better hurry. I've got a lot left to knit."

"You don't have to stay," Angie said to her.

Maddie looked up over her half glasses, startled. "And why wouldn't I stay?"

Angie flapped her hand vaguely. "You're tired...you've got the stock to take care of." She hesitated as if she might say more.

But Maddie forestalled her. "They're not more important than you," she said dismissingly. "I rang Taggart Jones before we left. He'll send some fellows over in the morning to see to things." She smiled. "It's the beauty of good neighbors. They come through for you."

Angie looked at Charlie. He could see in her face what she was thinking—that she'd never had neighbors like that. Until Chase and Joanna, neither had he.

He gave her hand a squeeze. "You've got 'em now," he said.

She smiled faintly, then pressed her hand—and his—against her abdomen. "Feel it?"

It was startling almost, the way it tightened like a drum skin right beneath his fingers. It made his eyes widen. "Whoa."

"Yeah." She ran her tongue over her lips. "You were gonna tell me...tomorrow...tonight," she corrected herself, "about you."

"Right." Charlie stretched and shifted again. "No time like the present. Besides, what else have we got to do?"

He wasn't used to talking about himself—wasn't comfortable doing so. The less people knew about him the better he liked it.

He'd only shared himself with Chase and Joanna and their family, the Cavanaughs and a few other close friends. He'd only shared part of himself with Cait.

He'd been too careful in those days, too wary of his own vulnerability. He hadn't wanted anyone to really know him. Cait had come as close as anyone, even though he'd held a lot back from her. He could see now why she didn't trust him.

How could you trust someone who didn't trust you?

Love meant sharing, he realized. It meant opening up and being vulnerable—at least to the people you loved.

He started to tell Angie. He didn't hold much back. It would be good practice, he thought, in case Cait ever let him talk to her again.

He told her about his father, about his mother, about Lucy. He told her about Chase and Joanna—how they'd pretty much saved his life.

"They wouldn't see it that way," he said. "But they don't know how close I came to falling right over the edge."

"Sometimes I think I'm falling over the edge," Angie whispered. Her eyes locked with his. Her lips were trembling.

He pressed her fingers between his. "You won't," he promised. "You won't if you don't let go. I won't let go of you."

But even as he promised, he knew the helplessness that Chase and Joanna must have felt. They had thrown him lifeline after lifeline when he'd been a teenager, but they'd never been able to make him hang on.

Ultimately he had to want to—he'd had to respond, to reach out to them.

He had—barely.

He'd been afraid to do more. He'd been afraid to let them adopt him.

What if they'd died like everyone else he'd ever loved? What if somehow it had been his fault?

That was, he realized, the reason he'd run from Cait. To save himself, yes—but also to save her and Resi.

Like he was somehow responsible for all the world's pain.

He wasn't. He could only do his best.

He gave Angie a lopsided grin as she tensed with another contraction.

"They're getting stronger, Charlie."

"Okay," he said, "let's go to work."

Five hours later it was time.

Cait checked on Angie frequently, but she didn't want to hover. It was her experience that laboring moms liked to have her nearby but not standing over them. It made them feel as though she was impatient and waiting to get on with it, and that it was their fault if nothing was happening.

And besides, there was Charlie.

Cait didn't want to be there with Charlie.

She hadn't wanted to call him. She hadn't wanted to see him. She'd told Angie they would do fine without him.

But Angie had insisted. "He said he'd help. He said he'd be here! He promised!" And with each sentence she grew more panicky and strident until Cait had had no choice but to call.

She didn't know if he'd come. She rather wished, for her own sake, that he wouldn't.

Of course he did.

She expected that he'd agreed to it so he could bother her some more, but it didn't take long for her to see she was wrong. She kept well away from him, of course. But for once he didn't pursue. His focus was entirely on Angie.

And before it was over, she had to admit it was a good thing he was there. He kept Angie steady. He kept her focused. He kept her calm. He talked to her almost nonstop in low, gentle tones that were so soft Cait couldn't really hear what he said even when she was in the room. And Angie listened intently to whatever it was he had to say.

When things began to speed up, when the contractions got stronger and labor more intense, he moved up behind Angie and let her grip his hands, all the while still talking to her, murmuring, steadying, encouraging, getting her to do what Cait needed her to do.

"I can't!" Angie cried at one point. "Oh, God! Oh, God! Oh, God!"

"Take it one breath at a time," Charlie said. "Work with me, Ang'."

And Cait could see their hands locked together, their gazes locked together. She could see in Charlie the man she'd once believed he could be—the man she'd wanted to marry.

But she had a baby to deliver. She couldn't let herself think about that.

"One more push, Angie," she said. "When you start to feel the contraction, go with it. Okay. Now. Push. Push!"

The girl grimaced, her sweat-streaked face red from exertion, her knuckles white from crushing Charlie's hands in hers. "I c-c-cannnn—I did!" she exclaimed as a wet squirming baby girl slid out into the world.

Cait caught her, held her, marveling as always at this miracle of new life, at the tiny perfectly formed fingers and toes, at the dark eyes that blinked at her.

Angie was crying, her body shaking with emotion and

exertion. Maddie was beaming. "Oh, isn't she lovely? Isn't she wonderful?"

And Charlie was just staring, an expression of awe on his face. Then he dropped a kiss on Angie's forehead. "Good for you, kid," he whispered.

Cait, watching, envied that kiss far more than she wanted to.

Denver.

She just had to get to Denver. That was what she told herself for the next twenty-four hours. Once she was in Denver—or even on the road—she would be looking toward the future, not the past. She would be seeing Steve, not Charlie.

And all would be well.

She kept telling herself that, counting the hours.

She wasn't sure exactly when she knew it wasn't going to work. Maybe she'd known before she ever set foot in Steve's car Friday night.

She'd jumped in eagerly enough, after giving her dad a hug and a kiss and the promise that she'd have lots to tell him Sunday night when they got back.

She'd refused to see the look of worry that had crossed his face. He was just concerned about himself, she told herself. He just wanted her to look after him forever. Well, she couldn't. If she needed to, he could move to Denver.

As for the weekend, she said blithely as she departed, "I'm sure Charlie will be checking in on you while I'm gone."

She was sure he would be. She'd asked him to. She'd made a point of telling him she was going when she'd seen him in Angie's room this afternoon.

She'd said, "Oh, by the way, if you could stop in and see Dad this weekend, that would be great."

He'd blinked. Then his eyes had widened and he'd

started to grin that heart-stopping Charlie grin, as if he thought she'd changed her mind and was going the long way round to say it.

So ruthlessly she'd gone right on. "Because Steve and I are going to Denver tonight to look for a place to live."

The grin had died, and she'd been pleased. It was an angry sort of pleased. She still felt angry.

"Who's Charlie?" Steve had asked.

"A new hand my dad hired," Cait said briefly. She was angry about that, too. She'd been dumbfounded when her father had announced that he was hiring Charlie.

"Hiring Charlie?" she'd said in stark disbelief. "For what?"

"To help out."

"He's not a cowboy!"

"He can dig a post hole well as most," her father said complacently. "And he's a damn good rider. He's got a good eye. Comes from takin' pictures, I expect. Don't matter. A feller's gotta start somewhere."

Cait didn't see why Charlie had to start at all. He was a photographer, for heaven's sake, not some two-bit cowpuncher! He'd leave again in a few days. Please God he would leave before she came back!

"You oughta be glad," her father said. "Gus said we need more help. Hell, sweetheart, you been sayin' the same thing yourself. Said you was overworked, you did. Needed more time for the hospital and the babies."

"Yes, but—"

"So, I hired Charlie, and now you got it."

Hallelujah, Cait had thought grimly.

But then she pushed thoughts of Charlie out of her mind. She breathed deeply. Steve stepped on the gas and they drove away.

Cait watched the ranch recede in the rearview mirror

and then, resolutely, she looked ahead. She waited for the feeling of anticipation, of euphoria, to settle on her.

It didn't come.

Miles passed. They stopped in Billings and got a bite to eat, then forged on. The sun set behind them and they turned south on 25 and before long headed into Wyoming.

Steve talked about Denver, about the new practice he was going to be joining, about the hospitals he'd be working at, about what neighborhoods would be nearby and where they ought to look for a place to live.

Cait didn't say a word.

She thought—about her father, about how hardheaded he was, how almighty stubborn. She thought about Angie and her baby. They'd checked out of the hospital today to go home with Maddie.

Angie still didn't know what she was going to do. She needed to find Ryan, the baby's father and talk to him. Cait had made her an appointment with Martha, the social worker, who might be able to help. Cait had mumbled words about adoption, in case Angie wanted to think about that but was afraid people would think she wasn't brave enough to keep her baby.

"Sometimes it takes a braver person not to," Cait had said. "You have to decide what's right for you and for...Charlene."

Angie had named the baby after Charlie.

Even Charlie had tried to talk her out of it, but Angie had insisted. "She's *my* baby," she'd said fiercely. "I can call her whatever I want. Her name is Charlene."

But she called her Charlie. Cait had heard her. She'd cuddled the baby close and whispered, "I love you, Charlie," to her.

Cait wondered which of them she was really talking to—the man or the child.

She tried not to wonder much. She tried not to think about it. About him.

About Charlie.

But it was hard. The trip was long. She was only marginally interested in Steve's ramblings about his practice. She wasn't interested in Denver. She didn't care where they lived.

Charlie, too, had held the child. He'd stroked her soft cheek with his finger, a look of pure awe on his face, a smile flickering, barely suppressed as he'd said softly, "You're a darn sight better looking than me, kiddo."

She wasn't.

No one on earth was better looking than Charlie. At least not to Cait. No one could make her heart zing the way he could just by walking into a room.

Looks weren't everything, she reminded herself sharply. Looks really didn't matter at all.

But it wasn't only Charlie's looks, the devil's advocate in the other side of her brain pointed out.

She fought with it. She turned away from her thoughts and stared out into the blackness. Steve droned on.

Cait thought about Charlie.

She couldn't stop thinking about Charlie.

Not that night. Not the next day. Not when Steve took her around the hospitals where he'd be working or to meet the doctors with whom he would be practicing. She tried to remember their names, tried to smile and be polite and friendly. But she felt disastrously out of place. Like her body was here, but her mind and heart were somewhere else.

With Charlie.

Damn Charlie!

She didn't want to feel this way about Charlie. She didn't trust Charlie. He wanted her—he said he loved her—but what did that mean?

It meant he wanted her in his bed. He wanted to be in hers. He wanted what they'd had in Abuk.

He said he wanted eternity, forever with her—but how could she believe him?

And why should she want to?

She had Steve! She loved Steve!

But equally, she knew she couldn't marry Steve—not when she was as mixed up as this. But she couldn't just blurt it out.

It wasn't that she'd changed her mind—it was that she didn't know her mind! She only knew that she was a fool to be planning a huge wedding to one man when she couldn't get another one out of her head.

So she kept her peace. All day Saturday she smiled and nodded and listened to the doctors Steve introduced her to and the hospital administrators they met. She did the same with Annette, the real estate lady who showed them through half a dozen condos and an equal number of houses.

"What do you think?" Steve asked her.

"What do *you* think?" Cait countered.

"I want you to be happy," Steve said. "You decide."

The real estate lady looked at Cait expectantly.

Helplessly Cait shook her head. She couldn't blurt it out here, either. "I don't know. I think we need to...talk."

That night at dinner she tried to find the words to say what she felt. "I think we ought to...hold up a bit," she said at last.

"Hold up?" Steve looked mystified. "You mean about picking a place? Well, that's okay with me. You know that. I just thought you might not want to move twice. We can rent an apartment. I can call Annette back and—"

"I didn't mean about the place. I mean about the wedding."

Steve stopped, his fork halfway to his mouth, and stared at her. ''The wedding?''

Cait shrugged helplessly. ''I'm just...confused.''

''About me?''

''No! Me! It's me,'' she said desperately. ''Not you. It's just...I don't know what to do!''

Slowly Steve shook his head. Lines appeared above his brows. ''About what?''

''About...life. About...love. About...what I want.''

It sounded so stupid, so shallow. She felt like a child—a badly behaved, selfish child. But what else could she say? It was the truth.

''I've been so busy. I've been worried about my dad. I haven't had time to think. And now there's all this planning and I...just...I don't think I'm ready. Yet,'' she tacked on desperately.

''Ah.'' Steve's brow cleared. ''Yet.'' He smiled a little. ''Prewedding jitters.''

''Yes!'' Cait grasped the explanation eagerly. Then she shook her head. ''Sort of.'' Because honesty required more than that. She didn't want to talk about Charlie, but she did want to let him know there was more to it than a few stray worries. ''I'm sorry. I just...don't feel ready. And I can't get married until I do. Do you see?''

Why should he? She wasn't making sense!

But he nodded. ''I think I do.''

She pressed her lips together in a moue of self-disgust. ''I'm sorry. I didn't realize until we came. Then it became so...real. I—'' She stopped. Then she began to struggle to pull off her engagement ring. ''Here. You shouldn't be stuck being engaged to a woman who doesn't know her own mind.''

But he reached across the table and stilled her hands.

"No." He shook his head and his eyes, cool blue eyes, steady blue eyes, smiled faintly. "Wear it."

"But—"

"Wear it," Steve said. "I want you to. You'll get yourself sorted out. And maybe is better than no."

Eight

"Been thinkin'," Walt said as they pushed several dozen head of cattle across a hillside, heading for lower ground, "'bout Vietnam."

"Uh-huh." Charlie wasn't thinking about Vietnam. He didn't give a rat's ass about Vietnam.

It didn't matter to Walt, who was talking more to himself anyway. "Thinkin' 'bout people I knew. Wonderin' what happened to 'em. People I ain't seen in years, y'know? Some people I ain't never seen…" His voice trailed off.

Charlie didn't fill in the silence. He was barely listening. He had his own preoccupations—namely Walt's daughter, whom he had last seen yesterday afternoon.

She hadn't spared him a glance. She'd been in Angie's room to give her instructions and advice to help with the baby. She'd talked to Angie—and to Maddie. She hadn't said a word to him.

She hadn't spoken to him directly since she'd called him to tell him Angie was in labor three days ago. All her comments had been directed at other people, even when he was the one the message was aimed at.

"I bet you could use some ice chips," she'd said to Angie during labor.

Get the girl some ice, she'd meant, Charlie knew.

"A back rub would probably help you right now, wouldn't it?" she'd said to the girl at one point.

She'd meant, *Rub her back, you fool.*

When Angie had been leaving yesterday, he'd been there, too. Cait had been full of compliments and sage advice, and she'd told Angie how well she'd done and Maddie what a great help she was going to be over the next few days and weeks. And then she'd said, "If you need anything, give me a call. Except, this weekend you'd better ring Dr. Ferris because I'll be out of town."

"Where're you going?" Charlie had asked.

But she'd just said, "Bye. I'll try to drop over to the ranch to see you next week." And she'd walked out without a glance in his direction.

She'd gone to Denver, he now knew.

Walt had said so when he'd come by last evening to tell Charlie they were moving cattle today. "You oughta come eat supper with me," he'd said. "Caity'll be gone all weekend," he'd grumbled, "Her an' Steve gone down to Denver. To look for a house." He hadn't looked thrilled.

Charlie wasn't at all thrilled.

He'd barely slept a wink last night thinking about her spending the night with Steve. His mind had whirled with memories of his own nights with Cait. He'd relived every wondrous, tender, explosive moment. He'd ached with longing.

He'd been ready to chew nails when Walt had shown up this morning about six to head up to where they were going to move cattle. Walt hadn't looked much more rested than Charlie felt. His graying hair stuck out in tufts beneath the brim of his cowboy hat. He had a day's worth of stubble on his cheeks and a hollow look about his eyes.

"You feelin' all right?" Charlie asked him. He didn't need Walt having a heart attack on him in the back of beyond.

"Ain't been sleepin' too good. Been thinkin'," Walt had said.

He'd been talking about his thinking ever since. Charlie had let it go in one ear and out the other. It was Vietnam, Vietnam, Vietnam—stuff about making decisions and having regrets and wondering if you did the right thing.

Charlie had enough of his own questionable behavior to worry about. He didn't have time to spare on Walt's.

They moved the cattle. It was about the sort of work Charlie needed. Semi-mindless. Physical. Demanding at times, brainless at others. It kept him busy, but still gave him time to think about Cait. And since there was nothing he could do about her, it spared him bouncing off the walls of the cabin in frustration.

He thought he'd be able to sleep that night. The day's work had been demanding. He should have been dead on his feet. He declined Walt's invitation to stop for supper and then head on down to the Dew Drop for a little refreshment, figuring he'd grab a bite at the cabin, then sleep hard and deep. But he ended up pacing furiously instead.

He decided he'd had too much of his own company, so he got in Otis's Suburban and headed over to Brenna and Jed's. If they were surprised to see him turning up on their doorstep at nearly ten o'clock at night, they didn't say so.

"Ah, reinforcements," Brenna said, actually looking relieved. "Here." And she handed him a fussy baby.

The baby's name was Hank. He seemed big compared

to Angie's newborn. A person already—albeit an unhappy one. Charlie juggled him nervously. "What should I do?"

"Walk with him," Brenna said. "It's what we do."

She and Jed slumped wearily on the sofa and gave him grateful smiles. Otis and Tuck, watching a baseball game on television in the other room, looked around and gave him approving looks.

"Why not?" Charlie said. It was what he'd been doing back at the cabin. Jed got up and poured him a beer. Charlie held Hank in one hand and the beer in the other and he paced.

Something about his limping gait must have soothed the baby, because it wasn't long before Hank's head nestled against his shoulder. The sound of his wails softened, then disappeared altogether. It was replaced every once in a while by a sigh and a tiny hiccup.

"He's got the touch," Jed said in reverent tones.

Brenna nodded. "Can Hank go live at the cabin with you?"

Charlie laughed, causing the baby to stir and fret just a little before he slept once more. "I wouldn't mind," he said. "But I think he would."

Jed and Brenna exchanged looks.

"Nesting instinct got you?" Brenna asked.

Charlie shrugged. He wasn't admitting anything. He didn't need anybody's pity because the woman he wanted was in Denver with another man.

Brenna seemed to sense that. She didn't press. She just let him continue to pace until it was clear that Hank was down for the count. Then she led Charlie upstairs to the baby's bedroom. "Here's the test of true power," she said. "Can you ease him into bed without waking him up?"

"I used to be pretty good with my friends, Chase and Joanna's, kids." He'd lugged a colicky Emerson around a lot of nights.

"Novel way to keep a kid off the streets," Chase had said with a grin at the time.

But Charlie hadn't minded. It had made him feel needed. It had made him a part of things—even when he'd insisted he didn't want to be a part.

He realized now how foolish he'd been. He realized how he'd been fighting himself all these years. It was nice to have finally got it straightened out.

Pity that Cait didn't believe him.

He laid Hank in the crib, and the baby gave a tiny shudder, but his eyes stayed shut. He made a soft sucking sound as if he were dreaming of nursing. A faint smile curved his baby lips.

"You're a miracle worker," Brenna breathed.

And moments later when he accompanied her back downstairs, Jed looked at him with real respect. "A regular genius," he said.

Charlie stayed with them until after midnight. He talked with Brenna about her next show at Gaby's which was coming up in the fall. He talked to Jed and Otis about the cattle he and Walt had moved today. He talked to Tuck about the Porsche and admired some of the drawings Tuck had done of it.

It was a whole lot better than rattling around the cabin by himself, worrying himself sick about Cait and Steve in some Denver motel room. He liked the company and the conversation. He felt comfortable. At home.

He wanted…

He wanted to stay.

Not simply at Jed and Brenna's. Not at Jed and Brenna's at all, really. But in Elmer. In the valley. Here. In this community. With these people.

With Cait.

"Getting tired?" Brenna said, smothering a yawn.

And Charlie, startled, realized how late it was and how

early Jed would have to be up in the morning—how early Walt would expect to see him—and how much he had overstayed his welcome.

He scrambled to his feet. "Hey! I'm sorry. I wasn't thinking. I just—" He shrugged, a little embarrassed at how he'd settled in.

"Glad to have you. Wish you'd come down sooner," Brenna said. "But I know you had your own priorities." She took his hand and gave it a squeeze. She was smiling at him.

Had Gaby told her why he'd really come?

Suddenly he didn't care. "Thanks," he said to all of them—and meant it from the bottom of his heart.

He slept.

Fitfully.

He dreamed.

Desperately.

He woke.

Haggardly.

Sunday was even worse. Walt woke him up when he finally fell asleep at dawn.

"Uh, right. I'm gettin' up," he mumbled, only to have Walt tell him he wasn't coming today, that he had things to do at home.

"Don't mean you can lie abed all day," the old man said. "Just that I trust you to do it yourself," he said. "Just ride that fence line along near the water hole."

It was a vote of confidence, of course. Walt believed in him. Another time Charlie would have been gratified by the news.

Today he could have used the company. Riding fence was far less demanding than moving the cattle. Far less interesting, too. And without Walt there to drone on about Vietnam, naturally all his thoughts were of Cait.

She would be back today. He would go down tomorrow and see her. And if she said she and Steve had put a down payment on a house, what was he going to do?

Was he going to battle all the way to the altar? Was he going to fight to make her love him? Or was he going to beat a tactful retreat?

They weren't questions he wanted to consider.

He didn't believe in retreats.

But he didn't believe in making Cait's life miserable, either.

He itched to call Chase and talk it over. But since he hadn't really followed the advice Chase had given him the last time they'd talked, he didn't think calling again and confessing he'd done the opposite would net him any stars for good behavior now.

Besides, whatever Chase said would probably be right—just as what he'd said last time was undoubtedly right. And Charlie would probably do it wrong. Again.

But he was beginning to get the idea that there were some things a guy had to work out for himself. Convincing the woman he loved that he did indeed love her was obviously one of them.

He finished with the fence about five in the afternoon and rode back to the cabin, passing the water hole as he went.

He didn't stop. He didn't need any more reminders. And even though he was hot and tired and his leg ached, he didn't even consider taking a dip.

He unloaded the pack horse, put away the wire and posts he'd taken along, then unsaddled his own horse and turned them both out to graze. He didn't even have to think about it anymore. Handling horses and fencing material was getting to be second nature now. The silence didn't bother him now. In fact it didn't seem all that quiet. There were birds. Grasshoppers. The rustle of the breeze blowing through the trees.

There were a lot of people in the world who wouldn't believe this was Charlie Seeks Elk if they could see him now. But he knew it was a good fit. A better fit for the man he'd become than going back to cover wars would be.

Yes, he could get used to this.

He could love it and never leave it.

If only he had Cait.

It was dusk when Charlie heard Walt's truck.

He was making coffee and, given Walt's unerring instincts and love of java, figured that the old man must have heard him pop the vacuum seal on the new can. Well, good. He could use the company. He hadn't spoken to a soul since Walt had rung this morning.

Maybe Cait was back. Maybe Walt had news. Charlie felt his insides clench. He got out a second mug, set it on the table and stepped out on the porch.

Behind him, over the Bridgers, the last light was fading. From the east the truck rounded the bend, and Charlie could see its headlights bouncing as it navigated the dirt track. He stood, one hand braced on the porch support and waited.

Finally the truck pulled up alongside where he'd left Otis's Suburban, and the engine shut off. The door opened.

"Coffee's on," Charlie called down. "You must have ears like an elephant," he added as a figure emerged and the truck door shut.

"Thank you very much," a decidedly female voice dryly replied.

Charlie's stomach did a complete flip.

"Cait?"

* * *

This was a bad idea.

A very bad idea.

An idea born of desperation and agitation and not much else.

But it was the only idea Cait had—so she had gone with it.

And now the time for backing out was past. The minute she'd driven through the gate and started up the hill, she knew she'd reached the point of no return.

He'd hear her coming. He'd be waiting. Expecting someone. She couldn't just turn around and head back down.

Well, she could, but she wouldn't let herself.

She'd lived in limbo too long. It was beginning to feel like hell. And she had to resolve things one way or the other. She couldn't go on like this.

It was Charlie's fault, she reasoned. So it was Charlie who was going to have to help resolve it.

Now she took a deep breath and walked resolutely toward him. "Yes," she said. "It's me."

She was close enough now that she could see the glint of his grin.

Don't, she thought. *Please, Charlie, don't!*

She didn't want him to be happy, to be glad to see her, to virtually welcome her with open arms.

"Hey," he said, still grinning. But when she didn't smile in return, gradually his grin began to fade. His brows drew together. "What happened? Did something happen to Walt?"

"What? No. No, of course not. I—" She raked a hand through her hair. She'd raked her hands through her hair a hundred times in the past hour, it seemed. "He's not even home. I don't know where he is."

And she was glad of it. It meant he was getting out,

doing things, having a life. And it meant she didn't have to tell him about her weekend in Denver with Steve. She didn't want to talk about it—or about Steve—or anything else for that matter, until she had things settled in her mind.

"Then...what?" Charlie was looking worried now. Good. She was tired of being the only one whose life was spinning out of control.

She stuck her hands in the pockets of her jeans and debated how to begin. Just baldly blurt it out? Work it into the conversation?

"I'll have that coffee," she decided abruptly. Maybe if she had a few moments to think things out...

Charlie blinked, then nodded. "Right. Come on in."

He went back inside, leaving her to follow.

The room seemed even smaller now than the last time she had come, when she had brought him the ice. Then it had been Charlie filling it. Now all she seemed to see was the bed. She jerked her gaze away from it.

Charlie was pouring two mugs of coffee. In his jeans and a navy-blue long-sleeved shirt, his black hair flopping forward onto his forehead, he looked healthy and handsome and comfortable in his surroundings. He looked as if he fit in, as if he was at home, as if this *was* his home.

Last time she'd thought how out of place he seemed here, but not now. The cabin had his mark on it—and it seemed to have made a mark on him.

It surprised her.

It disturbed her. She'd wanted him to hate it, to leave it. To go away.

He was adding a dollop of milk to one of the mugs. Hers. And then he carried it over to her. "Here you go."

"Thank you." She was careful that their fingers didn't touch. The mug was hot, but it gave her something to hang on to while she got her bearings.

Charlie had his bearings. He looked relaxed, one hip

propped against the sinkboard as he took a sip of coffee and regarded her over the top of the mug.

Cait studied the coffee in her own mug. Then she looked around the room. She shifted her weight from one foot to the other, breathed deeply and tried to find the right words. There were no right words. There was only the deed.

She looked up at last. "I want to go to bed with you."

So much for Charlie looking relaxed. His heels hit the floor with a thud, and he stood up straight so quickly that the coffee in his mug slopped onto his hand. He blinked rapidly, and a tide of color darkened his cheeks.

He opened his mouth, but it took a second or two for him to respond. It was as if she'd knocked the breath right out of him, which she supposed she had.

And then he said, "Yes," and started to grin. It was a warm grin, a wonderful grin. A grin of relief and joy.

Cait couldn't look at it. She gripped the mug between her palms and began to pace, shaking her head. "I didn't mean that," she muttered.

Behind her Charlie sucked in a breath. "What did you mean?" His voice was quiet. Without even looking she knew the grin was gone.

She didn't turn around until she reached the far wall and was forced to. Then she stopped and turned and lifted her shoulders irritably. "I meant that we need to sort things out...clear the air."

Charlie stared at her. "Sort what out? Clear what air?"

"Between us!" Cait shoved one hand through her hair this time. "Between us! It's making me nuts. I can't...I can't think! I can't make sense of things! I tried to find a house with Steve this weekend and I...I kept thinking about *you!*"

"What a shame," Charlie said dryly.

"It is," Cait said, frantic. "It's wrong! I shouldn't be feeling this way when I'm marrying someone else!"

"Or maybe you shouldn't be marrying someone else."

Damn him for being so bloody rational!

"I don't know what I should be doing!" She was almost shouting now. "Don't you see?"

She didn't wait to find out whether he saw or not. She went back to pacing again, almost knocking over one of the chairs. Charlie reached out and snagged it out of her way. She took a deep, steadying breath, then stopped and faced him again.

"I told Steve we couldn't get married the way I'm feeling right now. I told him I needed to clear my head. And this is the only way I can think to do it."

"By going to bed with me?"

"By getting you out of my system," she agreed. "And it can help you, too!"

"Really?" Charlie lifted a brow.

"Yes," she insisted. "It will get me out of your system, too."

He just looked at her.

It was what he'd wanted, damn it! It was *all* he'd wanted two years ago!

And here she was, standing in front of him offering it to him—offering *herself* to him—no strings attached.

Take me to bed.

How much more blatant could she be?

And Charlie shook his head. A faint rueful smile touched one corner of his mouth for just a moment, then it disappeared.

"I don't want you out of my system, Cait," he told her quietly. "I love you. So, thanks, but the answer is no."

Nine

He needed his head examined!

For crying out loud, she'd just flat-out offered to go to bed with him—and he'd said no.

Like he hadn't wanted to! Like it hadn't been the very thing he'd been hoping for and dreaming of since he'd come back from his encounter with eternity.

He had hoped for it. He had dreamed of it. Had prayed for it.

But not like this.

He understood now the old adage, "Be careful what you pray for," because when she stood right there and baldly offered it to him, he couldn't take it.

It wasn't enough.

He didn't want only Cait's body in his bed. He didn't want merely the softness of her skin against the roughness of his. He didn't want just sweet murmurs and shaking passion.

He wanted love.

God help him, he wanted her love.

But that wasn't what she was offering, and he knew it. So they had stood and stared at each other for what seemed like another eternity, but which could only have been a few seconds.

And then—when Charlie said no…thank you, but no—she'd turned on her heel and walked away.

And now he stood staring at her taillights as the truck hurtled down the hill. He braced one hand against the porch post, gripping it so hard he felt his nails dig into the wood.

"Damn it!" The words were wrung from him.

They broke—a harsh ugly painful sound echoing exactly the way he felt since the moment of his refusal when he'd watched the color drain from her face.

She'd blinked her astonishment—and her hurt—then carefully, oh, so carefully, she'd set her coffee mug down on the table, turned and walked out the door.

For at least ten seconds Charlie had stayed right where he was. Frozen. Not just immobile, but literally cold as ice from the inside out.

Then he'd heard the truck door open and slam shut. He heard the engine kick over, sputter and die. Then the key ground in the ignition and the engine growled to life again.

The sound had moved him. He reached the top of the steps in time to see her jerk the truck into reverse and back it around. He was conscious of her overrevving the engine. He knew she was angry as hell.

He just didn't know what he could do about it.

So he said, "Damn it," again. Then he took a breath. Short, shallow, all he was capable of—and he let it out.

"You can't do anything about it," he said quietly into the darkness.

Around the bend, the taillights disappeared. The sound of the truck grew fainter.

He waited. He listened. But in a few minutes, even straining, Charlie couldn't hear it anymore.

In the silence he stood alone.

Slowly he let go of the post, unbent his knuckles and saw his hand begin to shake. He balled it into a fist and jammed it into his pocket. His throat started to thicken and ache, and he swallowed desperately. His eyes began to burn and he shut them. He clamped his teeth together to trap and swallow the sound of pain. He stood there, rigid, fighting it.

But it was a fight he wasn't going to win.

It was over.

He'd been as honest as he could be.

She'd walked away.

So much for bad ideas.

Such a bad idea it was positively off the charts!

Anger, pain, mortification, humiliation.

Cait felt all of the above—and knew she deserved every one.

The emotions had come in waves. Anger first. She couldn't believe he'd said no. *Thanks, but no.* Like she'd offered him a piece of pie for dessert. Calm and almost dismissive. But polite.

God, yes! He was so freaking polite!

No, thank you, Ms. Blasingame, I don't want to go to bed with you. Her face could still burn just thinking about it.

The mortification and humiliation were in a dead heat for second.

The last time Charlie had, in effect, turned her down, he'd done it without saying a word. He'd simply got up in the middle of the night and left.

She hadn't figured it out right away. The realization that he hadn't just left for the moment, but for life, was gradual. And painful. And mortifying.

She'd felt such a fool.

She couldn't imagine ever feeling like a bigger one.

But she did now.

This time, like an idiot, she'd spelled it out. She'd flat-out offered her body to him—and he'd rejected her.

When would she ever learn?

No, that wasn't right. She had learned!

And then there was the pain.

It was the pain of rejection first. Then the pain of embarrassment and humiliation. Those were the feelings of pain that had propelled her out of the cabin, into the truck and down the hill. Those were the feelings that had roiled in her heart and in her soul and in her mind as she berated herself for her foolishness. Those were the feelings that kept her awake and pacing all night. Those were the feelings that wouldn't even let her face her father.

She heard him come in, but she pretended to be asleep.

She couldn't answer questions about her weekend in Denver. Her weekend in Denver seemed a million years ago!

And she couldn't tell him about tonight. She couldn't talk about Charlie to her father, who thought the sun rose and set on him.

So she huddled in the darkness of her room and relived the stomach-grinding humiliation of her evening with Charlie over and over and over.

She beat on her pillow. She punched and hammered it, then clutched it against her belly and wrapped herself around it.

And she wept.

For her foolishness. For her needs. For wanting a man she didn't want to want.

Then, as night slid into the first rays of dawn, the tears subsided and she lay silent and still and stared at the ceiling. And she realized that her foolishness was even greater than she'd thought it was.

Charlie hadn't refused to make love with her tonight to embarrass her or to humiliate her or even to hurt her.

He hadn't taken her to bed because he really did love her—and he hadn't been willing to settle for less.

Her lips trembled. Her vision blurred, and the tears came again.

But this time Cait wept for an even greater foolishness—for not believing him.

"You look like hell," Steve said when she finally tracked him down late Monday afternoon.

She hadn't had a chance before. She'd lain awake until dawn, aching and crying for herself—her foolishness—and for the man she'd lost by denying feelings she'd been afraid to have.

There was no reason to keep Steve's ring now. No sense in holding out the slightest bit of hope for them. But just as she was thinking she might call him, her phone had rung and it had been one of her patients telling her that she was in labor.

Cait had never felt less like doing her job. But she hauled herself up and headed for Livingston. She'd find Steve later. But between Lucy's labor and delivery and the patients she had appointments with at the office, she barely had a chance to think.

That was a good thing—as the only thoughts she had were of Charlie—and of what a fool she'd been. Well, she had the answer to her question now.

She was no longer confused about why she was thinking about Charlie when she was determined to marry Steve.

It was because she still loved him.

Charlie had been right and she'd been wrong. Terribly terribly wrong.

She knew that now—for all the good it would do her.

"I feel like hell," she told Steve frankly when she finally saw him. She tried to smile, but her mouth didn't seem to be working.

"What happened? It's not your dad?"

Everyone thought everything was her dad. But Charlie had helped him out of whatever depression he'd been in.

"It's not my dad," Cait said. "It's me." And this time she really did wiggle the ring off her finger and put it in his palm. "I can't marry you."

"Ever?"

She nodded, just once. "I can't."

"What did I—" he began but she cut him off.

"It's not you. It's me. And someone else," she added, needing to be honest because Joyce had seen that kiss. Joyce had heard her argue with Charlie. And she didn't want Steve hearing things she hadn't had the guts to tell him.

Steve looked at her. "Who?"

"A man I used to know. A man I thought I was over—and wasn't."

"And he came back for you?"

"He tried," Cait said. "I turned him down. But then I realized—"

Steve made a face. "And now you're going with him."

Cait shook her head. "No. Now I'm quite sure he won't want me."

"Then—"

"No. I don't love you the way I ought to. Seeing him again made me realize that. I would only make you unhappy. I'm sorry."

Steve smiled wryly. "Yeah. Me, too." He hesitated, then went on. "Though I'm not exactly surprised."

He didn't look exactly heartbroken, either. In fact, he looked almost relieved. Or maybe, Cait thought, she was just indulging in wishful thinking. She didn't want to ask what he meant. She'd behaved badly enough already. So she just looked at him and hoped he would explain.

"You kept making up excuses not to go to bed with me."

Cait shut her eyes. If she hadn't already used up her lifetime supply of mortification, she could have wallowed in it here. She ducked her head and shifted from one foot to the other. "I didn't mean…"

But she couldn't finish because obviously she *had* "meant"…or her body had. It had apparently realized what her mind had not—that Steve was not for her.

"I'm glad I'm moving to Denver," he said frankly.

"Yes," she agreed, looking up at last. "And I'm sure you'll meet someone there. Someone better for you. More suited. Someone who loves you the way you deserve to be loved."

Before he could answer, his beeper went off. He smiled a little ruefully, then actually laughed as hers went off ten seconds later.

He tucked the ring in his pocket, then reached out and gave her hand a squeeze. "Take care of yourself, Cait."

She clung for half a second, then let him go. "I will. You, too."

He turned and headed for emergency. She watched him go, knowing she'd done one right thing at last. Steve had his whole future ahead of him, and he would meet someone far better than she was. His future was bright.

Hers seemed endlessly bleak.

"I'm amazed. No, I'm not amazed," Gaby said as she studied the slides Charlie had spread out on the light box. "I mean, I knew you'd find something wonderful. And I knew you said mothers and children, bears and babies, but I never thought…'' She lifted her gaze and her eyes shone. ''They're brilliant, Charlie. They're just wonderful.''

''Uh-huh.''

Some of them had promise, he was willing to admit. The series on the mother bear and her cubs was strong. He'd done some good stuff on a horse and foal, too. And he had some he liked of Angie and the baby.

He'd taken quite a few of Brenna and her bunch while he was there. Those girls of hers, Neile and Shannon, were shot stealers, for certain. And he'd done a whole series of Brenna with Jed's nephew Tuck. He saw echoes of his own relationship with Joanna. Brenna was the closest thing to a mother Tuck had, and his devotion was clear.

They were both artists, and Charlie had taken lots of shots of them working, talking together, studying a subject, then working again. He'd taken other shots as well—of Brenna and Tuck on horseback, of Brenna and Tuck doing dishes, of Brenna sitting in the passenger seat of his Porsche and Tuck behind the wheel, pleased as punch to be driving her to town in such a vehicle.

But perhaps his favorite shot of all was one of the whole family around the dinner table—Jed, Brenna, Otis, Tuck, Neile, Shannon and Hank. Three generations. A complete mix: Brenna's father, Jed's nephew, her child by her first marriage, the two they'd had together. Laughing, arguing, talking.

Family.

Loving. Caring. Supporting.

It made him ache just to look at it.

It was what he'd always wanted—even when he'd been afraid to reach out for it—first with Chase and Joanna, then with Cait.

Yes, he'd finally come to his senses. But with Cait the hurt had been too deep, and he'd left it too late.

There was a moral there somewhere. Charlie saw it staring him in the face.

He regretted leaving Montana, he was grateful for Brenna's offer to come back whenever he wanted and he said maybe someday he would.

After all, Cait wouldn't be there. She'd be safe in Denver with Steve. Or if she didn't marry Steve, she'd find someone else. Someone who got it right the first time.

Not him.

"We can hang a show next week," Gaby said now, eyes shining.

"What!" That was impossible. Shows took months to set up. Charlie stared at her, mouth open.

She laughed. "Not a full-scale, all-out, one-man band sort of show. But I've got a show opening next week—Nathan Wolfe. You know Nathan. He does those fantastic arctic photos. Animals. Birds. He's got some wonderful polar bears. What you have here could blend in." She was warming to the notion, he could see it in her eyes. "Your own audience will find you, anyway, but since you've moved on in your interests, you're going to want people to know where you've gone. Nathan's audience would be a natural."

"Nathan won't be thrilled." A man didn't happily share a one-man show.

But Gaby disagreed. "I think he might. He's been a bit distracted lately." She shook her head. "He keeps muttering about having other things on his mind. Like he thinks I don't? Anyway, he hasn't given me all I need to really go big with this, so if we hung some of yours—just a couple of series even—you'd fill my walls and you'd be doing him a favor."

"I don't know..."

Gaby, of course, took that as a yes. She was already picking the slides she wanted to use.

And Charlie didn't have the energy to argue with her.

He didn't have any energy at all.

He had come back home two days ago, and he'd done nothing since he got here except stare at the ocean.

It didn't have the soothing effect it usually had. It was too…flat.

He still liked the horizon, but he didn't like it flat anymore. He needed a little high relief. He needed mountains. Towering pines. Icy, running creeks.

Southern California felt alien to him. He'd never been so aware of the pollution, the noise, the buildings, the cars. There were so many people. Too many people.

And not one of them was Cait.

It always came back to Cait.

He had to stop thinking about her. He had to get past it. He'd given it his best shot. There was nothing else he could have done.

You could have gone to bed with her one last time, he told himself. If he had, at least he would have had the memory. But maybe that would have been worse.

He tried to tell himself it would have been worse. Sometimes he believed it. He needed to stop thinking about it.

"Fine," he said heavily to Gaby now. "Do it. I'll help."

Maybe it would distract him, occupy him, force him to get on with his life.

She finished picking the slides she wanted. Then she went into his kitchen and made them both a cup of coffee. When she had poured it, she sat down, and for the first time she looked at him and studied him as closely as she'd studied his slides.

"You're not happy."

"No."

Her eyes softened. Her expression saddened. "The woman in Montana…"

"Is still in Montana," he said flatly. "And I'm here."

"Ah, Charlie." Her eyes reflected his misery.

He shook it off. "I'll get over it."

She touched his cheek. "Of course, Charlie. Someday you will."

She would get over it—over *him.*

She had to. She had no choice. It wasn't as if she could go running after him now. She'd made her bed, as her father would say. She would have to lie in it.

And she did. Miserably. Night after night. With all the memories of what might have been.

Every day Cait dragged herself out to work. She saw patients. She helped mothers and fathers bring babies into the world. And when she had the slightest bit of energy left, she threw herself into work on the ranch.

They needed her help since Charlie had gone.

She wasn't surprised to hear that he had.

Her father was.

"Thought he was comin' into his own," he'd said, shaking his head when he'd told her. "Told him he had the makin's of a pretty fine hand."

"He's a photographer, Dad. He has a job to do."

"He was doin' it here," Walt groused. But then he stopped, straightened up and squared his shoulders. "Glad he came," he said. "Made me think about things I hadn't thought about in years."

Cait wasn't really listening. She was thinking about Charlie as always.

She was completely shocked, then, to come home from work a few days later to find her father packing a bag.

"Dad?" She stopped at the doorway to his room and stared at him.

He jumped as if she'd surprised him. Then a fleeting embarrassed smile flickered over his face. "Oh, Caity. You're home, then."

"I'm home. Are you…leaving? Taking a trip?"

She'd encouraged him to get out, to do things, to bounce back from the heart attack, to find new interests if the ranch wasn't enough. But he'd never said he was going away.

Had he?

She'd been in such an emotional funk since the night she'd had her encounter with Charlie that she didn't hear half of what anyone said. "What are you doing?" she asked him.

"I wouldn't have left without telling you," he said now, folding a shirt and laying it in the bag.

"Well, good." She tried a smile. "Of course you wouldn't. Are you taking one of those weekends to Las Vegas? Going to see Aunt Rachel in Seattle?" Please, God, don't let him be going to California to visit Charlie.

He straightened up and faced her squarely. "Vietnam."

She was conscious of her jaw falling open and her eyes widening a lot. Vietnam? No, she was quite sure now—he'd never told her that.

"But…why?"

"Now that's somethin' we need to talk about." He left the bag sitting on his bed and crossed the room to her. "Come sit down. I want to tell you a story."

An army story?

Her father had never been one of those guys who spent hours talking about his experiences in the military. He didn't live in the past. It was over, finished. Whenever she and Wes had asked him about those days, after they had heard about Vietnam from their friends or their friends' dads or they had seen something on television, he'd brushed them off.

"It's over," he'd always said brusquely. "Time now to move on."

Of course his sentiment was shared by a lot of people.

For one reason or another, many did not want to look back at what had happened in Vietnam. Her father had simply been one of them.

Until now.

Now he told her his story.

Cait knew some of it. Her mother had told her about their long-distance love affair. ''I wanted to get married before he left,'' she'd told Cait. ''But Walt wouldn't do it. He said he didn't want to leave a widow. And he said I was too young, that I might meet someone else. As if I would.'' She'd shaken her head and laughed at the chance of that.

Cait had understood. Her father was still, at sixty, a handsome man. And when he wanted to he could charm the ladies. But the only woman he'd ever looked at, as long as Margie was alive, was her mother.

''Margie was so young,'' he told Cait now. She sat on the sofa where he'd steered her while he paced back and forth. ''A child. Nineteen, for heaven's sake. And she thought the world rose and set on me. She never knew anyone else! She never,'' he reflected, ''wanted to know.''

He paused and ran his fingers over his short, salt-and-pepper hair. ''I thought we should wait. War's unpredictable. I didn't want her tied to me. We wrote letters. She was a lifeline to the world I knew. I loved her for it. I loved her,'' he said more firmly. ''But I was surprised when she actually came to Hawaii for my R&R.''

That part Cait had heard about. She knew lots of stories about the whirlwind week her parents had spent together on Oahu. Her mother had told her time and again, her eyes shining, of how exciting it was to see her father again, to touch him, to hold him.

''Of course she came,'' she said now. ''Why wouldn't she?''

''Lots of women didn't,'' her father said. ''Guys went,

hoping…and their girls weren't there. I was all ready to have the same thing happen to me. I couldn't believe it when I got off the bus at Fort DeRussey, and she was actually there.''

''She loved you, Dad. She would never have gone with anyone else.''

''I know that now. I knew it in Hawaii. I didn't know it before.''

Cait stared at him, not quite following.

He didn't say anything for a long moment. Then he sighed and spoke, his voice low. ''I met a woman in Vietnam. A teacher. Before I met your mother in Hawaii. Before we got married. This teacher spoke some English. She wanted to learn more.'' He rubbed a hand against the back of his head. ''She asked me to teach her.'' He stared away out the window again.

Cait didn't have to guess what had happened next.

She remembered Abuk. She remembered Charlie. She knew exactly what could happen. It had happened to her.

''Her name was Sue. Well, actually it was somethin' I never could pronounce,'' her father said ruefully, ''so I called her Sue. She was a fine woman. And I…I—'' He stopped and shook his head, unable to say the words.

''And you fell in love with her.''

He twisted his head to look at her. ''I don't know if I loved her or not,'' her father said, surprising her. ''I liked her. I liked her a hell of a lot. I might have even thought I loved her. She was sweet, funny, generous. Very kind to a homesick American guy. But then I went to Hawaii, and I saw your mother again and there was no comparison. That was love, Caity. That was my future. And when I went back, married, I looked up Sue first thing and I told her so.''

He turned away again. Stood still as a statue. And Cait contemplated him. She tried to envision her father as a young man in a foreign country, finding solace with another woman. She could see that. She imagined even her mother might have understood. They hadn't been married, after all. And once they'd got married, he'd presumably ended it with this Sue.

"And you never saw her again?"

He shook his head. "I told her we couldn't."

"And now you're going back to look for her?"

"Not for her, Caity. She's gone. She died several years later. Right at the end of the war."

"But then...?" She didn't understand.

A ghost of a sad smile touched his mouth. "There was a child."

Cait couldn't move.

She was glad she was sitting down. She stared at her father as if she'd never seen him before.

A child?

Her father and this Vietnamese teacher, this woman called Sue, had a...*child?*

There was another Blasingame halfway across the world? A half brother or sister of hers and Wes's? A sibling she had never known?

Never even heard of?

She tried to bend her mind around this. "All these years..." Her voice trailed off, her mind whirling. "A child?"

Her father nodded. "A child."

"Did Mom...?"

He knew what she was asking. "No. No one knew. I never said."

"But—"

"Life is full of choices, Caity. We make them, sometimes on the spur of the moment, sometimes with a lot of thought. But we make them—and then we go on. We do the best we can with what we've made. It's what I tried to do.'' He sighed. ''I didn't know Sue was pregnant when I left for Hawaii. Had no idea. Hadn't even considered the possibility, fool that I was. I didn't find out until I came back and told her I was married.''

''Oh, God.''

Her father sighed. ''Yes. Oh, God. I was pretty well poleaxed when she said. I didn't even want to believe her. But I did.'' He studied the tops of his boots, then lifted his gaze and looked straight at her.

''But you didn't see...you never knew your—'' Cait couldn't even finish a sentence.

''No. I let it go.''

''You never—''

He shook his head adamantly. ''No. I might have been able to try to get the child. I might have been able to claim it and have brought it to the States. Some guys had kids there and did that. I didn't. Sue wanted to keep the baby. She said so. And I...I didn't push. I was afraid to hurt your mother. I didn't know what she'd say. I was afraid to...rock the boat. Afraid to take the risk.'' He sighed and slumped a little then, as if the decision weighed him down.

''But why now?'' Cait asked.

''Because when I had that heart attack last fall, I had a lot of time to think.''

That's what he'd been thinking about? That's what had made him so pensive and withdrawn?

''And I thought I could die without ever having known him...or her. Because I wouldn't take a risk.'' He shook his head. ''I'm not saying I was wrong in the first place, Cait. Maybe I was. Maybe I was selfish. I was damn sure scared. So I made the choice I thought was right—and I went on. I didn't look back.''

She tried to think back over all the years of her life, all the years her father had lived keeping this inside him, tried to imagine what it must have been like for him to walk away from this child he would never know.

"But I'm looking now," he said. "It was your little gal that made me start thinkin' I needed to look."

Cait started. "My little gal?"

"The one in Charlie's book. The little girl in the hospital. The little girl who lost everything in the war. Seein' her made me think. It made me feel guilty, and like I needed to know. I talked to Charlie."

"Charlie knows?"

"Charlie and I have talked. Not about my…my child. About kids. About risk. About war. About life. About dyin'."

Cait nodded. Yes, Charlie knew about dying. Her throat grew tight. Her eyes blurred.

"Reckon I might never know," Walt went on resolutely. "It might be impossible. There might be too little to go on, it might be way too late. But I don't want to die without tryin', Cait." His pale-blue eyes met hers. "I don't want to die without tryin' to find 'im. Eternity is a long long time."

As usual Gaby pulled out all the stops.

The night of the opening, the sangria flowed and the champagne corks popped. Critics and journalists drifted along with art patrons who had more money in their checking accounts than Charlie would earn in a lifetime, casually consuming trays full of Santa Fe's trendiest hors d'oeuvres while they wandered through Sombra Y Sol's gallery rooms, murmuring and discussing the photos, Nathan's and his.

It was Nathan's show, of course. Nathan would be the one the critics praised or scorned. He was the one whose work they would buy or walk away from. He would live or die by the results of it.

But Nathan barely seemed to care.

He was distracted. Preoccupied. Forgetful.

"We're lucky he even remembered to show up," Gaby muttered, glaring at him. "At least he could have dressed for the occasion!"

Nathan was wearing jeans and an open-necked shirt. He was standing with the same half-full glass of champagne that Gaby had handed him an hour ago. He looked startled when one of Santa Fe's biggest art patrons came up to talk to him. Watching, Gaby groaned.

"He'll be all right," Charlie said.

"Will he?" Gaby didn't look optimistic. "He's about as bad as you were a few months back. Couldn't follow a three-word sentence from beginning to end."

Well, yes, Charlie could do that now—if he worked at it.

He'd been working at it. He'd been trying hard. Working his butt off to help Gaby get the show hung. Determined to take his mind off Cait.

It was true what he'd told her—that he didn't want to get her out of his system. But he had to function.

If he wasn't going to have her in his life, he still had to live. He'd come back to Santa Fe with Gaby the day after she'd proposed the show to him. He'd been working flat-out ever since. It was how he coped.

But it wasn't easy.

His mind could still drift away in the middle of a conversation. He could still see a flash of dark hair in the other room, and if the light caught it just the right way, he would still whip his head around to see if it might be her. Some voices had nearly the same timbre as hers. Some laughs were almost, but not quite, as genuine and delighted.

Some woman someday would probably come close.

But no other woman was Cait.

He'd hoped Joanna and Chase would say something encouraging, something that would give him hope.

He'd gone to see them as soon as he'd got home. He'd walked straight into their house and put his arms around both of them and said right out, "Thank you for everything. For being there. For…loving me."

It hadn't even been hard to say it, though he'd thought it might.

And the looks on their faces—the joy, the tenderness, the love—had made him wish he'd had the courage to say it, and to believe in it, years ago.

They loved him. They told him so. But they hadn't held out hope for him with regard to Cait.

Joanna had hugged him and told him with maternal ferocity that Cait was crazy. Chase had clapped an arm around his shoulders and said, "It's hell, man. I've been there."

He had. But at least Chase had found his way back.

Eventually, Charlie reminded himself, years later Joanna had found him again.

So maybe…

But thinking things like that was the way to drive himself nuts.

"Ah," Gaby said, patting his hand and craning her neck to look past dozens of gallery lurkers and patrons, "your family's arrived."

And Charlie looked around, following her gaze, eager to catch a glimpse of Joanna's red curls and Chase's raven hair. He'd told them they didn't have to come.

"It's not a big deal," he'd said. "Not a one-man show or anything."

"It's your show," Chase had said.

"It's a big deal," Joanna had said. "We're all coming."

That meant they were bringing the kids, too. He was glad. For all that he'd said they didn't have to come, he was glad they had. He'd looked forward all week to them coming. He wanted them all here.

Now he could hear seven-year-old Annie's high-pitched voice saying, "Look, Daddy. Look! There's Charlie's bears!" And he saw her tug Chase to see the bears Charlie had told her about, but not before Chase had nodded backward toward the rest who were following him.

Charlie spotted the ten-year-old twins, Emerson and Alex. They waved to him, gave him a thumb's-up, then made a beeline for the punch bowl and the food.

Then he saw Joanna. She caught his eye and smiled, then drew someone else forward.

Cait.

Charlie stared. The noise faded. The clink of glasses, the clatter of trays, soft comments, raucous laughter, droning opinions—all of it—vanished. The only thing Charlie could hear was the roar of blood in his veins.

Cait?

Here?

He blinked, disbelieving. But when he looked again she was still there. Looking straight at him. There was a warmth, a tenderness, a hope in her eyes that he remembered from the days she had first loved him.

It was the expression he'd looked for on the day he'd been shot, when he'd sought her out in the crowd of people in the light. The day she hadn't been there.

And now she was here.

He felt a deep, fierce ache in his throat. He felt his body begin to tremble.

"Charlie!" Gaby's voice sounded a million miles away. "You're spilling that champagne!" Then her gaze seemed to follow his and she said quietly, "Oh. I see."

He felt her grab the glass out of his fingers and take him by the hand and pull him across the room, through the throng of people to where Joanna stood with Cait.

She didn't say anything when she got him there. And he didn't, either.

He couldn't. He didn't know what to say.

Cait did. She wasn't smiling as she looked at him. Her eyes were brimming. "Forgive me?"

"For what?"

Her lips trembled. "For being a fool. For doubting you. For being afraid."

He was the one who was afraid now—afraid he was hearing things, seeing things—afraid to believe.

"Afraid of what?' His voice sounded rusty.

"Of loving you. I do," she said, and it sounded like a vow. "Oh, God, Charlie, I do! And I believe you love me, too!"

A pinch-faced critic stepped between him and Cait. "I've been looking for you, Mr. Seeks Elk. We need to discuss this unpredictable highly irregular turnabout in your work."

"I—"

Cait was looking at him, her heart in her eyes.

"You are the one who did those stunning post-urban chaos photos, are you not?"

"I—"

Her fingers reached out tentatively past the critic to touch his. His wrapped tightly around hers, and he gave her his own heart, though she'd had it all along.

"I find the departure astonishing," the critic rabbited on, regarding Charlie over his spectacles with blatant disapproval. "And not a little disconcerting. I wonder how you can move so rapidly from such brutal realism to this…this…tender, hopeful…" He said the words as if they were epithets.

"I—"

"Can't," Gaby finished for him firmly as she took the

man by the arm and drew him away. "But I'm his agent and I'll be happy to talk to you."

The critic was only slightly mollified. He shot a look over his shoulder at Charlie and Cait.

Gaby made shooing motions at them with her hands. "Go on," she mouthed. "Go." Then she tucked her arm into the critic's and led him away to see the mothers and the babies—the bears and the horses and the humans.

"How do you account for this astonishing development?" the critic demanded.

"Well," Gaby said, "I think it all began when he saw the light."

He had her in his bed.

He had her in his arms.

Just as, for so long, he'd had her in his heart.

He couldn't believe it. He'd had to keep stopping on the walk back to the apartment just to touch her, to kiss her, to reassure himself that she was really here.

"I'm here," she'd said. "I'm here." But there was such wonder in her voice, that he guessed she didn't mind reassuring herself, too.

"I was so wrong," she told him when they went inside and shut the door. She wrapped her arms around herself, hugging herself tightly, fiercely, shaking her head, and then she looked up at him anguished. "I'm sorry. I do love you."

And all Charlie could think to tell her was the truth. "I love you, too."

Then he wrapped her in his arms and held her close. He didn't kiss her this time. He just held her—felt the warmth of her body melt the ice that had held his heart so long, felt the gentle touch of her hands against his back, felt them press him closer. Felt their two hearts begin to beat as one.

"How did you...Chase...Joanna?"

"I went to find you. You were gone. So I went to find them. Joanna wasn't all that thrilled to see me. She told me a few home truths." Cait smiled a little ruefully. "And I deserved every one of them."

"Joanna can be a little fierce," Charlie said, smiling as he stroked her cheek.

"She loves you."

"Yes."

"I love you, too. I don't want to get you out of my system, either, Charlie," she whispered. "I understand about eternity now."

His hand stilled and he looked deep into her eyes. "Do you?"

She kissed him. "Oh, yes."

He took her to bed then and he loved her.

His body ached for release. But he made himself go slow. He stroked her skin. He kissed the line of her jaw, the slope of her breasts, their peaks and the valley between. He moved over her, touching and brushing. His hands shook. His body trembled. He reined it in.

He was making memories. He was storing up pieces of eternity.

Until finally Cait wrapped her arms around him and drew him down and into her warmth. He felt her body clench and heard her cry out. And he closed his eyes and saw the light—and gave himself up to their love—and to her.

They had more than time now.

Their love went beyond.

Charlie had never seen snow.

"Never seen snow?" Cait had been astonished when he'd told her that. It had been September then. They'd come back to the ranch from their honeymoon in Jamaica to find two inches of snow on the ground.

He'd shaken his head. "Never." And he'd scooped it up in his hand, oddly surprised when it felt so cold. He'd tried packing it into a snowball, but it hadn't worked. He wasn't skilled at it. Something else he'd had to learn.

Now it was December. He could mend a fence now. He could spot black leg and scours. He could make a snowball. And a snowman. And he could shovel it for hours.

"Never saw so much snow in my life," he muttered as he stood with his arms around his wife and watched a blizzard of white flakes swirl around outside.

"You haven't seen much snow," Cait reminded him, laughing. "Remember?"

"I've seen enough," Charlie said darkly. "Seen one snowball, you've seen 'em all."

"Think so, do you?" Cait challenged.

"You bet." He tugged her toward the door. "Want to have a little snowball fight?"

"You just want to show off, now that Tuck and Jed have taught you all they know," Cait said.

"Well, yeah."

And he wanted to go outside and roll around with her. Actually he wanted to go to bed and roll around with her, but it was only two in the afternoon, and Walt would look askance if they disappeared upstairs.

They were living at Walt's for the moment, deciding whether they would build or if Walt would. He'd come back from Vietnam with leads, but so far nothing had turned up. They were waiting. Hoping.

"I'm a little nervous," he conceded.

"It's worth the nerves," Charlie told him. If he hadn't gone back after what he'd left behind, he wouldn't be here now. He wouldn't have Cait.

"Just a few snowballs?" he said now, grinning at her.

Cait shook her head. ''Can't. We have obligations. *You* have obligations.''

The Elmer Christmas pageant, she meant. When he'd married Cait, Polly McMaster had let them have the town hall for the reception rent free, with one string attached—Charlie would direct the town's Christmas pageant.

''She won't expect me to come today! It's dumping out there.''

''Haven't you ever heard the old adage, the show must go on?'' Cait teased.

''But—''

''Come on. The sooner we get there, the sooner we'll get home.''

It wasn't true, but Charlie wasn't going to argue. He'd have his way with her sooner or later—and anticipating it was almost as sweet.

It snowed the rest of the afternoon. It snowed into the evening. It didn't matter. Everyone within ten square miles of Elmer, Montana, attended—as they always did. No one got stuck in the ditch. No one delivered a baby on stage. Charlene, whom he'd cast as the babe in the manger, never whimpered, Angie whom he had coerced into playing Mary, actually sparkled. And when it was over, he was quick enough to avoid getting stuck bringing home all the rabbits that had doubled as livestock in the manger.

Grinning as they went out to their truck, Cait told him he was learning.

He laughed. ''Yeah, I guess I am.''

Sometimes he thought he had so much to learn about life and about love that he would never touch the surface of it. Sometimes at night he woke up and just lay looking at the love of his life and marveling that he'd been given another chance.

Sometimes she would wake to find him lying there and, wordlessly, she would understand and wrap him in her arms. She would love him—and he would love her—and they would come together, two hearts, two hopes, two souls made one.

They would do that tonight.

But first they ate a late supper. Then he helped Walt with the chores, and while Cait brushed out her hair, he called Chase and Joanna and regaled them with the tale of his directorial triumph. Then she finished and turned to smile at him, a look of such love in her eyes that his heart seemed to catch in his throat.

"Gotta go," he muttered to Chase. "Take care. Love you all," he said to Joanna.

Then he hung up and took his wife in his arms.

Outside the snow continued to fall. Inside they were safe and warm. Cait drew him down with her onto the bed. She kissed him.

"Remember once," she said, "when we were in bed and I started talking about love and marriage and family."

"The first time, you mean?"

She nodded.

"I remember."

"And you were scared."

"Yeah."

"And now you're not?"

"You'd better believe I'm not," he vowed. "Marrying you is the best thing that ever happened to me. I promise you that."

"And the rest?" Cait persisted.

"What do you mean? Love? You know I love you. Family?" The light suddenly dawned. It glimmered. Or it could have been that tears were blurring it. "Caity?"

She laughed and rolled together with him on the bed, and he held her gently, reverently, and heard words he'd never thought he wanted to hear and knew now were his greatest joy.

"August first more or less," his wife the midwife told him, "you're going to be a father."

* * * * *

Anne McAllister's dynamic miniseries,

THE CODE OF THE WEST,

will continue with her exciting new single title,

THE GREAT MONTANA COWBOY AUCTION

On sale January 2002.

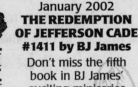

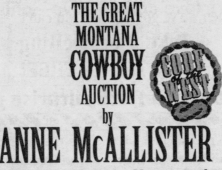